FIRE & LIES

Windtree
Press

OTHER TITLES

FIRE & LIES

PAMELA COWAN

Windtree
Press

Copyright © 2020 Pamela Cowan

All rights reserved.
ISBN-13: 978-1952447211 (Print)
ISBN-13: 978-1952447204 (eBook)

Windtree
Press

818 SW 3rd Avenue, #221-2218
Portland, OR 97204-2405
855-649-0821

First Edition
Printed in the United States of America

DEDICATION

To Jim

My husband. My best friend.

My pandemic buddy.

ACKNOWLEDGMENT

I would like to thank my sister, and the inspiration for this novel, Barbara Duncan. Like El and Em we share a childhood, a dash of sibling rivalry, and a love for good puzzles. My daughter, Jeanne Bainbridge-Chavez, a devilishly-cruel editor, who turns craft into art. My neighbor and friend, Mark Runnels, retired ADA, not only for his insight into the inner workings of a DA's office, but for his wonderfully twisted take on crime and criminals. Finally, thank you to my friend, author J.M. McCracken, president of the Northwest Independent Writers Association, for the time and support you unfailingly provide.

CHAPTER ONE
Sunday, September 9

The sharp smell of gun solvent filled the air, a scent out of place in the tidy home with its traditional furnishings and dated bric-a-brac. Dodge, who had inherited the house from his recently deceased mother, would never have been allowed to clean his guns inside while she was alive.

Humming softly, he paused to say, to no one in particular, "I love the smell of gun oil in the morning."

After he unloaded each gun, he lined them up on the dining room table. Picking up the cleaning rod, he took a square patch of cotton rag and dipped it in Hoppe's solution. Then he poked a corner of the fabric through the rod's eye and tugged it halfway through.

The dining room table was covered with an old red and white checkered tablecloth lined with a thin layer of felt. He used it plastic side down and the gray felt was dotted with dark specks and trails of oil from years of use.

All five of his guns were on the table awaiting their turn. There were two rifles, a .270 Winchester, and a .30-.06 Springfield he used for deer hunting, as well as three of his favorite handguns, Glock 19s. They were matte black and all business. He'd once owned four, but things happen.

He picked one up and forced the cleaning rod through the barrel. It came out clean. Hadn't fired that one in a while. The second was the same, but when he ran it through the third, the clean white patch came out gray with carbon.

Tugging the dirty patch free, he dumped it into his makeshift rag bin, a tin turkey pan he'd bought for cheap at the dollar store, and decided to disassemble the weapon and do a thorough cleaning.

There was a pleasant calm that settled over him when he cleaned his guns. He imagined it must be how an ancestor might have felt sitting at the fire, a leather strap across his thigh, while he notched flint into arrows. He could almost imagine the flickering of the flames and the smell of smoke.

Even if he hadn't fired them, bugs, dust, and humidity couldn't be ignored. It was his custom to clean each of his guns on Sunday morning. "Regular as church," his mother always said, and then she'd laugh like the batshit crazy thing she was.

Once the gun was clean, he grabbed a tube of lubricant and put the smallest drop on the rails. It was a new product. Smelled of sage. He got some on his fingers and rubbed them together. Liked the slippery feeling. Suddenly he was struck by an idea.

Taking the tube of lubricant with him, he went to his bedroom. The girl was tied to the headboard by her wrists and to the footboard by one ankle. There was just enough slack for her to move, but not enough so she could untie herself and sneak out.

"Got a surprise for you," he told her as he kicked off his boots and dropped his jeans. He squeezed a few drops of the expensive lube into his palm, then rubbed it up and down the length of his penis. "You're gonna like this."

She was shaking and her eyes tracked his every movement as he walked toward the bed, but his overnight guest didn't say a word or make a single sound. Fast learner, he thought, smarter than her mother at least.

Not that he expected smarts from any of the pale men or women who lived in Jansen's Mill. The Mill was nothing more than two rows of single-wide mobile homes on a rutted dirt road. Loggers had lived in the temporary quarters for a short time but had abandoned the place in the seventies. Two miles from the highway, in the middle of an old clear cut, it sat just outside the reservation. From the highway, the place looked like piles of discarded, rusting junk. Up close it stunk of failed septic systems, rotting garbage, and despair.

There were times Dodge and his friends talked about burning the whole thing to the ground, just to improve the air quality. They didn't mind poor folks as a general rule, but these people were beyond poor. Jansen's Mill was the last step before homelessness for a lot of miserable drunks and drug addicts.

Unfortunately, Dodge's business, which was moving methamphetamine, heroin, and whatever else he could get his hands on, counted on the people who lived there. They were not just his best customers, but also willing mules and unwilling, but easy to use, scapegoats.

He looked down at the girl. She had long straight brown hair still sweat plastered to her head from their last session, big brown eyes, and an average face with just a sprinkle of acne along her jaw. She wasn't his type: too thin, too white.

On the other hand, that white skin was tight and smooth as only young skin can be. He figured she had to be thirteen, fourteen tops.

Kicking his jeans free, he climbed onto the bed and reached for that silky skin.

Afterward, Dodge was so spent he figured he might as well let her go. He got up and got dressed first though. Didn't pay to turn your back or be vulnerable around these pale girls. They could turn on you quick, use their teeth, or anything else they could get their hands on. This wasn't his first rodeo.

He stomped his feet into his boots, then went to

the girl. There were signs of loving on her skin, red splotches on her pale skin and a huge hickey on her thigh.

Her eyes were shut tight and that was fine for what he had to do next. He drew back his fist and threw a quick right. Not too hard. He didn't want to break any bones in her face. He just wanted to give her a nice black eye, one that would last a bit. She shrieked and moved away as far as the ropes would allow, staring at him as wide-eyed as a startled colt.

"Stay still," he said curtly. "I'm trying to untie you, damn it." He worked the knots free and unwound the rope from around her wrists. "When I snap my fingers, you'll get up and get your clothes off that chair there," he said, nodding at the rocker in the corner of the room. "Then you'll get dressed. Once you're dressed you'll walk to the front door and head home. As soon as you get home, I want you to tell your mother something. Do you hear me?"

The girl nodded.

He moved to the foot of the bed and tugged the slip-knot free, then unwound the rope he'd wound around her ankle. She didn't move.

"You tell her that she's going to remember not to short me next time. I don't mind the trade she made this time, but you're the only kid she's got, so she's out of things to barter. From now on, I want cold cash."

For a moment Dodge let himself feel sorry for the kid. Had she been a child of his people, her mother would have cut off his dick before she let him touch her. These pale women would sell anything. More proof that their souls were broken. Maybe his mother hadn't been all that crazy.

"I'm sorry I had to hit you," he told her. "It's not that you weren't worth the money, it's just that your mom's a stupid sort of woman, so she's gonna need a lot of reminding. Now, every time she sees your face, she's gonna remember."

The girl had turned away and was looking down, her long hair acting as a drape to hide behind. He put his fingers under her chin and lifted her face so he could examine the eye. Hate to have to hit her again, but no, it was starting to swell, the eyelid drooping so that in an hour she'd only be able to see out of the other one. There was a teardrop-shaped bruise forming near her nose too. It was going to be a beauty.

He stepped back and snapped his fingers.

As he watched her slip through the house and out the door, her narrow hip bumping into the doorframe in her stumbling haste, he almost regretted turning her loose. Almost. Women were a distraction and he had things to do.

After she left, Dodge cranked up his favorite country radio station. He was tapping his foot to George Strait's, "All My Exes Live in Texas," as he set down the last rifle and leaned back to admire his work. All his guns were still arranged along the table because he liked the look of them. He'd get around to putting them away after lunch. Or maybe he wouldn't put them away. This was his house, after all.

He was headed to the kitchen, to heat up a can of chili and dig a bottle of Keystone out of the fridge, when he heard the low but discernible creak of loose boards. Someone was walking across the front porch. The radio must have drowned out the sound of them coming up the driveway.

There was a trio of sharp taps as someone rapped on the door with their knuckles. Had to be a neighbor or a friend. Salesmen and peddlers of religion never trekked out this far. Maybe Jelly, his second in command, was dropping by. Jelly didn't like phones. They had that in common.

"Goddamnit, every time I'm busy," he cursed under his breath. But it was just a routine gripe. He didn't really mind the interruption. The prospect of company was not completely unwelcome.

He opened the door.

The bore of a 12-gauge shotgun is around two-thirds of an inch or about the size of a quarter. To Dodge, it was as wide and dark as the hell he was surely headed for. So focused was he on seeing and identifying the threat that all his other senses were muted. He neither heard nor, to his great luck, felt the blast of the gun, or the steel pellets that tore through his face and out through the back of his skull.

He was already dead as his body staggered back and fell against the heavy dining room table. From there, he slid to the floor, and came to rest flat on his back, arms spread wide, palms up. His forefinger twitched as if he were dreaming that he held one of his guns and was firing.

For a short time, blood poured from his head, pumped from his body at one hundred and fifty adrenaline-charged beats per minute, then it slowed as his heart gave one last squeeze and stopped. He became as still as only death can be.

Blood spread in a widening pool, soaking into the crevices between the old, well-polished floorboards.

CHAPTER TWO
Friday, September 7

Burned stuff stinks, and a lot of stuff had burned inside the warehouse. Emma could make out the harsh stench of melted insulation, charred wood, something chemical and probably toxic. She wondered if she should be wearing one of those masks, the kind firemen wear. But that was probably not necessary.

A cool autumn breeze was blowing through the place, all the way through. After all, there was nothing to stop it. The big garage door at the front had been shoved up and now hung at an odd angle. It didn't look like it would be coming back down any time soon. The rear wall was gone, and the row of windows that lined both sides had been blown out, either because of the heat, or the force of water gushing through fire hoses.

The floor was still damp in spots, but that might have been from rain getting in. After all, it had been over two weeks since the fire.

Standing at the center of the cavernous space, Emma turned slowly, trying to take it all in. She thought the warehouse must have been nearly empty when it burned. To the right of the front door, if you were facing the building, about a dozen scorched metal barrels—the ones her twisted mind always thought of as big enough to hide a body in—lay on their sides. Scattered among them were smaller metal containers, some round, some rectangular, all with their labels burned away.

On the other side of the warehouse, leaning precariously away from the wall, was the skeletal metal frame of a large shelving unit. The only remains of the wooden shelves were triangles of charred wood in some of the corners, and the sodden lumps of ash that wind and water had swept to the edges of the room.

Emma turned her attention toward the cans and the tell-tale trio of V-shaped marks on the wall above them. Fire burns up in a V-shaped pattern. The apex of the V is usually the point of origin. Multiple seasons of "Rescue Me" and other crime-based dramas had taught her that much. Still, despite her broad television-based education, she wasn't feeling very confident.

Her boots crunched through thin shards of glass from shattered fluorescent bulbs that had fallen from the ceiling. Each step sent up puffs of acrid ash that drifted lazily in her wake. She stood and stared at the row of dark V shapes as if waiting for them to speak. They didn't say a word.

Her friend and newest client, Gwen, had called yesterday afternoon.

"There was a fire at a warehouse on Market Street a couple weeks ago. We hold the policy on it and will have to pay off, unless it was set on purpose, which is what I suspect. Problem is, Devon and I are in Hawaii. We won't be back for another few days, so I can't go check it out in person."

"Don't you have investigators for that?" Emma asked.

"Yes, and the state police sent an investigator. Neither of whom found evidence of arson, but I don't know. Something doesn't feel right."

"How can you "*feel*" anything? Aren't you a couple thousand miles away on a beach with your boyfriend?"

Emma could sense the smile in her friend's voice. "Okay, you're right. It's not a feeling so much as I remember the guy who bought the policy. He came into the office when I was there, and he was scruffy as hell. I remember thinking at the time that he wasn't the kind of person I'd expect to buy insurance, especially on a warehouse that hadn't been used in years."

"So why'd you sell him the policy?"

"He said he was going to clean the place up and rent it out. He had a deal with a heavy equipment company that needed a place to work on their machinery. It sounded reasonable at the time. You know, protect the renter's stuff, protect himself from the renter."

"I don't know," said Emma. This kind of thing is not really *my* kind of thing."

"You *are* a private investigator aren't you? Go investigate."

She *was* a private investigator, but her specialties were finding and following. Her tools were a computer with a good internet connection, a camera with a zoom lens, and the ability to fit in wherever she was. She tried to explain that to Gwen.

"I'm not an arson investigator. I'm not sure I'd even know what to look for. If the actual investigators are saying it's not arson . . . "

"They're not saying it's *not* arson. It's more they're saying fire of unknown origin. I hate unknowns, don't you?"

"Of course, but again, this is not . . ."

"I know. Not your thing. I get that. But you have a way of knowing things, a gut feeling, Uncle Dan called it. You found Jason for him and he hasn't forgotten it."

Gwen's Uncle, had hired Emma to find a grown son he hadn't, until recently, known existed.

After following a twisting path, most of which took place across the Internet, Emma had found his son working as a pilot in California.

Dan, ex-Navy and a former airplane mechanic and Jason, his new found son, were still exploring the strange coincidences in their lives and flying around the country just for the hell of it.

The woman who had been Dan's childhood sweetheart, and the mother of Jason, had hated the idea of forcing Dan to marry her. Instead, she'd kept her pregnancy secret and moved away to live with her older sister. She'd had the baby and raised him, eventually marrying and later divorcing Jason's step-father.

Years later, when she thought she was dying of cancer, she decided it wasn't a secret she wanted to take to the grave. She'd found Dan and told him that he had a son.

Now, her cancer in remission, she often flew with the two of them. Emma thought the three of them might end up being a family after all.

"I'm not so sure about having gut feelings," Emma told her. "Usually all my gut tells me is that I'm hungry, but if it will make you feel better, I'll go poke around."

Gwen had then revealed more of what the firemen had discovered. For instance, that there were accelerants in the building but that this was not, by itself, suspect. The warehouse had once been used by a paint store to store everything from cans of paint to paint thinner and linseed oil.

They told her that linseed oil, with an ignition point as low as 120 degrees, was the most likely cause. If a can were knocked over, or had rusted and begun leaking, it could have given off vapors. The day of the fire had been clear and sunny. With all the windows and the metal roof, it could have become hot enough for the vapor to ignite.

Emma shivered as a gust of wind blew through the warehouse. Its icy touch reminded her that the sun was going down and taking all the warmth with it. She pulled a flashlight out of her jacket pocket and snapped it on. Then, going back to the front of the building she began searching in a grid pattern. As she walked, she slowly swept the light across the stained concrete floor. She didn't really need the light yet, for now it was just a way to help her focus on one thing at a time.

When she reached the barrels and small, what looked like one-gallon paint cans, she searched the area around them. Then, with the toe of her boot, nudged each so it would roll away, allowing her to see what was beneath.

It was slow, dusty work and she started to regret her choice of footwear. The boots she was wearing were fairly new and not cheap. They were starting to get crusted with ash. Would it trash the leather? Would she make enough on this job to replace them if it did? She doubted it.

Deciding to spare her boots, she knelt and used her gloved hands to continue the exploration. When she pushed at one of the smaller cans it didn't roll away easily, the way the others had. She lifted it and saw what had kept it from rolling. A small lump of black plastic on the concrete floor. When she tried to pick it up she found it was stuck. Cupping her hand over the palm-sized object she pushed side to side and back and forth until it broke free. She turned the object over and saw that two keys were embedded in the plastic, which must have melted around them from the heat of the fire.

"Interesting." The sound of her voice was tiny in the echoing space. Aware of the gathering darkness, she dropped the object into her jacket pocket and continued her search.

CHAPTER THREE
Friday, September 7

A few hours later, Emma sat at her sister's dining room table, staring down at the key fob. "What do you think, El?"

The girls had been born two years apart, Ellen first, then Emma. Their parents began calling them El and Em when they were toddlers, and though the girls fought it as teenagers, the nicknames had stuck.

Ellen turned the key fob over and peered at it closely. "Yep, it's definitely shaped like a car. Look, it even has windows." She ran the tip of one short, unpolished nail along a fine crack that ran in a perfectly straight line along one side. "Has to be for some kind of car."

"Well duh," said Emma, rolling her eyes. "But what

kind of car? An expensive one, right? It's pretty fancy. And what was it doing in that old warehouse?"

"And what do these keys open?" Ellen said, adding her own question to the list. Picking up a steak knife from the table, which was still littered with the remains of last night's meal, she slid the point under one of the keys and twisted. With a tiny screech both popped free. A small chip of black plastic fell to the table but otherwise the fob remained intact. "Look like house keys to me," Ellen said, turning them this way and that, but getting no further information.

"What's that?" Emma asked, pointing to a white mark on the fob that had been hidden under the keys.

The sisters bent close. The light above the table made the highlights in their dark brown hair shine a warm reddish gold. Aside from the identical color of their hair, and the squareness of their faces, there was little to mark them as sisters.

Emma was shorter and curvier than Ellen. Her hair was worn longer, with wispy strands framing her face. She also wore makeup, eye shadow, dark brown liner around dark brown eyes, and a shade of lipstick she'd worn since high school, something called

Cinnamon Rose, which she felt naked without.

Ellen had the athletic build of someone who likes to climb rock walls or run a few dozen miles each week just for fun. She had her hair cut, when she remembered to, in a short bob. She rarely wore makeup, unless you counted Chapstick, yet still managed to Emma's unending annoyance, to look as if she always put in an effort.

Bringing the fob closer, Ellen tried to make out what the white mark was. She shook her head. "It's some sort of emblem, I think, but it got ruined by the heat. You know, these doors look like they'd pop right off. Wait a minute."

Ellen, continuing to use the tip of the steak knife, began to carefully pry the fob apart. When Emma saw what she was doing, she said, "Hold on," then went to the kitchen, and returned with a paper towel. She laid it on the table and as Ellen removed each of the doors, Emma placed them neatly on the paper.

"Look, there's some metal things here. They look like they might be hinges." Again, using the knife tip, Emma opened each of them. The fob fell in half, revealing the electronics inside. Ellen continued to remove components, handing them to Emma, who arranged them on the paper towel.

They both stared down at the disassembled parts.

"Thirteen pieces," said Ellen.

"Fourteen, if you count the chip you broke off," said Emma. "But why would you?"

Ellen shook her head, barely suppressing a smile. "You would not," she said. "I'm not sure exactly what taking that thing apart got us, though."

"Not much. I was hoping there was another emblem inside, but no such luck."

"So, that means we have no idea what kind of car it's for."

"Not necessarily. I got on my cell phone before I came over and did a search for car-shaped fobs. I found out only a few companies use them: Porsche, BMW, Tesla, and Lamborghini, for instance. All fancier, high-end cars. It tells us that whoever lost their keys in the warehouse probably wasn't some homeless guy that broke in and accidentally set the place on fire."

"Probably not, but how do you know they lost the keys?" asked Ellen.

"What do you mean?"

"Well, what if they didn't lose them? What if they intentionally tossed them inside expecting them to melt in the fire? I mean, think about it. If you were planning to burn the place down, would you show up in your own car, or steal one?"

"Damn it," said Emma, "I didn't think of that. It could still be there, parked nearby. I'm stupid. I was so focused on the scene in my head I didn't consider anything else. I'll have to go drive around and see if I can find it."

"Only it probably isn't there anymore. It's been a few days since the fire, right?" said Ellen. "That's an industrial area. They won't let a car just sit there for days on end. They'll have it towed."

Once again, her sister had proven she was smarter. Emma wondered if humiliation could be fatal. Hoping her face wasn't reflecting her feelings she said, "Tow companies. Good idea. I'll call around. Why aren't you the P.I.?"

"Funny, but I never ask myself that question," Ellen replied.

Emma crossed her arms defensively. "I hate this. I agree with Gwen. My gut says that the fire wasn't an accident, but if I can't find something more than that key fob, I won't be able to help her prove it. I feel bad even billing her. Maybe I shouldn't."

"Don't start that. Gwen's got the money, and she hired you to give her your thoughts, not to solve the crime. What kind of business are you running? It's not your fault if there isn't anything to find."

"I guess," said Emma with a shrug. She was grateful, as she'd been hoping her sister would disagree and help take away some of the guilt she felt for taking on a job that was beyond her.

"Hey, you said it yourself," said Ellen, picking up on Emma's mood. "This isn't your kind of thing."

"That's the truth. I wish I knew an expert who could look at this," she said, staring down at the disassembled key fob. "Someone in the FBI would come in real handy about now."

"I know someone in the FBI," Ellen offered.

"What?" Emma said, surprise, and a touch of doubt in her tone.

"In fact," said Ellen, pointedly ignoring her sister's skepticism, "I have a friend with the CIA, one with the DEA and at least two with the US Marshall's Service."

Emma must have looked astonished, judging by the smug smile that crossed Ellen's face. "B-b-but how?" she asked.

"Where do you think ex-MPs go when their military service is over? Law enforcement, of course."

"Huh. I guess I never thought about it before."

"Well, duh," Ellen said, reaching for her phone. "I wonder which one of my friends can get the fastest results."

CHAPTER FOUR
Sunday, September 9

Willy's truck bounced down the narrow dirt road, in and out of shallow ruts and over rocks half hidden by grass and brush. The truck was heavily loaded and didn't handle well. The front tires felt like they were floating, or at least barely touching the ground, which made it hard to steer.

It was morning, not that early, but cold as a dead witch's tit. The truck's heater was acting up, blasting warm air for a moment and then ice cold. He rubbed his hands together, then grabbed the wheel as the road tried to send the truck into a shallow ditch.

What he was doing was probably stupid, but his uncle had died almost a year ago and his widow and their kid weren't doing so well, or so he'd heard.

They'd moved from Hollis out to Jansen's Mill so that pretty much proved the rumor.

His dad hadn't liked his brother, Gordon, and Willy had only met his uncle and his family once, at a funeral.

He remembered his aunt as a short, chubby woman with red hair, and his cousin, who was maybe five or six then, as a quiet kid who sat in the corner drawing with crayons. So, when someone traded him a load of split firewood for a pair of snow tires, he didn't know why he thought of them, but he had. It only took one phone call to track down their address. Out in the country, people usually don't share information unless they know you, but everyone knew Willy.

He finally reached the house, one in a row of small mobile homes, and backed in, careful not to hit the station wagon that had about as much rust and as many dents as the house.

As he climbed out of the cab, a woman stepped out of the house. She stood on the uneven pile of cinder bricks that served as her front porch and steps. He thought she might be his aunt, but he wasn't sure. Her hair was sort of the same, but instead of being a little bit chunky, she was a whole lot thin.

He went to the back of his truck and she glared at him for a moment, then said, "You're Willy, aren't you? You're William's son. What are you doing here?" Her eyes moved across the firewood piled in the back of the truck. "I never called you. I don't have money for wood." She stood half turned toward him, as if ready to jump back inside if she had to. The wind swept her across her face. She was blade thin, so skinny he half-expected the next gust to blow her off the porch. Maybe that was why she kept one hand on the screen door handle. "I don't have any money," she repeated.

"I know," Willy told her.

"And I don't take charity," she said proudly.

Willy had to turn away to hide his cynical look. When he turned back, he was all business. "I don't run a charity," he replied. "But someone gave me this load of firewood and I've got more than I can store. I figured I could barter with you. People almost always got something to trade."

His father had taught him that. He'd also taught Willy his favorite mottos: "You don't earn, you don't eat." "No good deed goes unpunished." "People suck." He would not approve of Willy not only giving away firewood, but spending gas money and tire tread delivering it. Willy didn't plan to tell him.

"Something to trade," she said. Then her puzzled expression slowly changed to a smile that he realized was meant to be seductive. She put her hand on one bony hip and said, "I might. You want to come on in and get warm?"

Holy hell, was she offering what he thought? She was his fucking aunt, even if it was only by marriage. When he mentioned trade, he'd been thinking maybe she could clean his house, or cook him a meal or something. Jesus. He almost jumped into his truck and took off. Then a new gust of icy wind reminded him why he'd dragged all that wood out here in the first place.

Sighing, he shook his head. "My girlfriend would put a bullet in me."

"She wouldn't need to know," Leena coaxed.

"Oh, she'd know," She's got some special kind of radar." He wasn't sure he liked this fictitious girlfriend. She sounded like she might be a special kind of crazy.

"Well," she said, giving up like it was second nature. Why don't you come in and look around;

maybe I have something that would be worth something to you."

"Sure," said Willy, though he was doubtful. Based on the pick marks on her face, the supermodel thin body, and the gap where her left canine should have been, Willy figured she'd traded anything of value long ago.

When he stepped inside the trailer, he knew he was right. The space was small but still echoed. There was nothing but a recliner that leaned to one side and a loveseat that looked as if it had been dragged from the landfill. Its arms were so shredded the wood frame showed through. A couple of blankets and a water-stained pillow marked it as someone's bed. At least it looked like someone kept the place swept up. It wasn't much, but it was something. Maybe Leena wasn't completely gone, or maybe it was the kid who was trying for something more than a needle.

To the right, beyond the living room, was an open kitchen and dining area. A table with a dollar store plastic tablecloth and two plastic chairs patched with silver duct tape were the only furniture there. A girl was sitting at the table eating cereal from a plastic bowl. Her long hair covered her face, but Willy knew it had to be his cousin.

"Hey Bonnie," he greeted her. She looked up, an unwelcoming scowl on her face. "It's me, your cousin Willy. You probably don't remember me." He was startled to see she had a black eye. Her eyelid and the area around it were dark purple, while the white of her eye was a vivid red. "Damn, what happened to you?" he asked, striding across the room, propelled by concern and a bit of morbid curiosity.

Bonnie half raised her hand as if to shield herself, then seemed to think better of it and lifted her face to him. "Running in the forest," she said. "Ran into a tree." She looked to her mother for confirmation and her mother nodded. Bonnie turned away to refill her bowl from a large generic bag of multi-colored flakes and went back to eating almost robotically.

"Running with her eyes closed," Leena explained. "Some new game the kids are into. Didn't we all do dumb things as kids? We used to hyperventilate and pass out, or sit in the back of someone's truck and find the worst roads, just trying to buck someone out. It's a wonder any of us ever survived."

Willy nodded. "That's true. Hey, you know, I just had an idea for a deal we could make on that firewood. How about this summer you let Bonnie wash my truck for me? It gets pretty muddy when I start hauling potatoes and what not. I'd pay twenty bucks a time. Three times would pay for that wood. What do you think?"

"It sounds like a good deal to me," said Leena. "What do you say?" she asked her daughter. "Do you want to do it?"

"Sure, I guess," said Bonnie, with no enthusiasm.

"Well, it's a deal then," Willy said. "You think you could give me a hand with the wood?" he asked Bonnie.

"I could help," said Leena.

"I just need someone to mostly hold the door open," Willy explained. "Plus, I was sort of hoping you could make me something hot to drink, coffee, tea, whatever you have."

"Of course. I've got some powdered hot cocoa. Would that do?"

"That would be fine. I imagine you want the wood stacked up along that wall there?" He indicated the area near the fireplace where the floor was deeply scratched and dented. No one would leave their wood stacked outside in this neighborhood. It would disappear in the night like socks in the dryer.

"Yes, please," Leena said.

Bonnie finished the last of her cereal and got up to help. Together they walked out into the driveway and the icy wind.

"Help me get that tailgate down, would you. You'll need these." He reached into his truck and from the front seat grabbed a pair of worn leather gloves. "Here," he said, as he helped her slip her small hands into each of the oversized gloves.

When he was done, she looked up at him. As soon as they locked eyes, he said. "Now tell me what happened to you, and don't lie. I've had enough black eyes to know the how of what happened. Now I want to know the who."

CHAPTER FIVE
Sunday, September 9

After talking to Bonnie, Willy had driven up along Deer Bone Creek and pulled over. Now he sat in his truck breathing as hard as if he'd run a fast mile. "Don't lose your shit." he told himself. "Think." He dug an empty Altoids tin out of his glove box, opened it, and picked out a fat green bud. He'd traded an old washing machine for the tin and its contents, and knew he'd got the best of the deal. He packed a pipe, lit up, and took a lung-filling draw. He had to relax, chill out. Think.

While Leena was making hot chocolate he'd kept grilling Bonnie, "Look, you're blood. That means I gotta look after you. Tell me how you really got that black eye. Your mom hit you? Somebody at school?"

"Mom never hits me," Bonnie said, in a tone that sounded a lot like bragging. "She got in trouble with her boss is all. He told her if he could have sex with me she could keep her job. She asked me if it was okay and I said it was. She didn't know he was gonna tie me up or punch me."

Willy shook his head but he wasn't really all that surprised. Loyalty was the first thing you learned out here. Defending family against other people, the law, the government. It was the same reason he'd driven out here, hauling wood for a woman he didn't know, but who had married into his family. It was what you did. Still, it made his stomach hurt. Pressing his thumb against his lower lip he chewed on the inside of his mouth, a nervous habit. "Okay, she didn't know he was gonna hit you but she knew he was gonna—ah hell."

"Yeah, she ain't winning no mother of the year award, that's for sure," Bonnie agreed, with a passive acceptance that broke his heart.

"Who's your mom's boss?" Willy asked, already fantasizing ramming his truck through the window of some fast food place, or beating the crap out of some guy at a gas station. The only job he could imagine for

Leena was waitress, or gas jockey, or something she could do on he back.

"Dodge," she said.

Willy's imagined scenarios disappeared like a puff of gun smoke. His heart hammered as adrenaline blew through his body, flooding his brain and muscles with oxygen and glucose, preparing him to run or fight. He didn't want to do either. Or he wanted to do both. He wasn't sure. So he smacked his gloved hands together and said, "Well, let's get to work."

They unloaded the firewood in what seemed like record time. Either it really did go quickly, or time had decided to speed up. It was like when he had a test back in school. Even though it was supposed to be a week away it always seemed to sneak up on him.

"Your drink's gettin' cold," Leena warned him. She was in the kitchen, he and Bonnie stood beside the wall of firewood in the living room.

He could barely make himself look at her. "Changed my mind," he said. "Give it to Bonnie would you? I just remembered I got some beer in the truck and milk and beer don't mix."

"Well, I guess not," she said, with a lighthearted lilt

that made him want to slap her lips off. "Though I just mixed water with the chocolate. There shouldn't be any milk in there."

Willy didn't even raise his eyebrows at the stupidity of the woman. He had much bigger issues with her than her intelligence, and it was taking all he had not to call her out for what she'd let Dodge do to Bonnie. The only thing that stopped him was the realization that using logic on an addict was as dumb as cooking with a wooden frying pan.

For a moment Willy considered walking over Deer Bone Ridge to Dodge's place. It would be faster than driving, but he didn't trust Leena not to sell his truck while he was gone.

Without the load of firewood, his truck rode better, and he pushed it hard getting away from Jansen's Mill and the nasty woman his uncle had married. The tires chirped as he left the gravel and bumped onto the asphalt highway.

Willy thought about his parents for a moment. His mother had died when he was too young to remember her. His best memories of his father were going out duck hunting with him. Before he could lift a rifle, he'd been the retriever, running into the marsh to find dead or wounded birds and bring them back. It was the most fun he could remember having as a kid.

His father, William Keene, known to the locals as The Banker, had a lockbox welded to the floor in the cab of his truck. Inside, he kept thousands in cash and a tidy stack of IOUs. That was why Willy knew exactly who Dodge was and how to get to his place.

Dodge's mother had been one of his father's best customers. A woman who always paid her debts when the tribal money came in. Over the years Willy had been out to their house with his dad at least a dozen times. Getting there wasn't the problem. The problem was—what the hell did he think he was doing?

Digging under the front seat, he came up with a bottle of whiskey. Putting it between his legs, he drove one handed while unscrewing the top, which he set on the seat beside him. He took a big swig, his eyes teared up and he wiped the back of his hand across his mouth. Then he took another slug.

His pickup drifted a bit and he had to steer back into his own lane as a huge diesel, hauling two trailers full of logs, roared by. A few minutes later he turned onto Muddy Creek Road, headed toward Dodge's and an increasingly uncertain future.

By the time he reached Dodge's place, a ranch on the south boundary of the reservation, he was drunk enough to have to concentrate hard to keep his truck on the road and not in the ditch.

When he reached the house he saw an old truck parked by the barn and Dodge's well-known black Camaro sitting out front. Willy swung the truck through the parking lot and backed up alongside the Camaro, leaving plenty of room between the two vehicles. He was still sober enough to know he might need to make a quick getaway.

Dodge had a reputation as a drug dealer with a violent streak. There were rumors about things he'd done that could make you sweat, but the few times Willy had talked to the man he'd seemed decent enough. At least he'd always had a big welcoming smile for The Banker.

Willy wasn't planning to get in a fight. He just wanted to talk to Dodge man to man, neighbor to neighbor, so to speak. Folks who had lived on or near the rez for generations had to stick together. Folks who lived at Jansen's Mill did generally get thought of and treated as trash. Dodge probably didn't even know Bonnie and her mom were related to The Banker. He didn't know Willy had been keeping an eye on them. He'd explain to Dodge that they were family and that he, Willy, would appreciate it if he kept his goddamn hands and his dick away from his cousin.

Willy's hands tightened on the wheel. He sat a moment and tried a little self-talk. Wouldn't do a bit of good to lose his temper. Better to have a plan, maybe offer some sort of trade. There was always something people wanted. Spare parts for the Camaro? Something else?

Then he realized what he had to do. Pretend he didn't know what Dodge had done. Let him know that Bonnie was his cousin, and more importantly, The Banker's niece. She was family, and you don't want to piss off The Banker.

He'd ask Dodge to keep an eye out for her, tell him that The Banker was concerned about her. That should get it across to Dodge, with the least chance of Willy getting his ass kicked. Willy wondered if he should add that The Banker didn't consider Leena family. The truth was, he didn't give a damn what Dodge did to or with Leena. Then he realized that was just anger and too much whisky talking. Just let that go. Keep it simple.

Could he sell it though? Was it the best plan, or was there a simpler, easier way to deal with Dodge?

CHAPTER SIX
Monday, September 10

Emma got to her office late on Monday. It didn't matter. There was no one there to care. A definite plus for being the owner and sole employee of Richland Investigations.

She'd spent the morning driving circles through the industrial area and surrounding neighborhood near the warehouse, just as she had the night before, with the same result. Her calls to the two local tow companies had resulted in the same outcome. Exactly nothing. No fancy car seen or towed.

Falling into her familiar routine, Emma grabbed the mail from the box outside the door. It had been delivered Friday but she'd worked from home that day, wandered around in the burnt out warehouse early that evening. Working not just when, but where she wanted, was yet another advantage of being her own boss.

She tossed the mail on her desk. Next, she hung her jacket and scarf on the slightly tilted brass coat rack the last tenant had left behind. After that: coffee. She filled the Keurig with water from the tap, risking an eventual mineral build up but enjoying the act of defiance. Her ex had been a fanatic about using only distilled water. It was worth the cost of a new coffee maker to thumb her nose at him on a daily basis.

Emma's office was in a narrow one-story building along a wide covered alleyway perpendicular to Main Street. Her office was the last in line so received more natural light than the rest, which still wasn't much.

Better, but not great light, was about the only thing the space had going for it. The view of the parking lot and of the brick rear wall of the US Bank building was certainly nothing to brag about.

The office was a fourteen-foot square room, with a row of metal file cabinets across the back wall covered with pots of gangly philodendrons. They were the only house plants that could survive in the dim space.

At the center of the office stood a large oak desk. Behind it was the ergonomic desk chair she'd splurged on. It was covered in buttery soft, light-brown leather. Facing the desk were two red leather guest chairs.

The wall to the right had a narrow buffet that held a coffee maker, an electric teapot, and all the paraphernalia that went with them. The wall to the left held a poster of Barney Fife from the "Andy Griffith Show," and her framed Oregon private investigator's license, as well as the door to the restroom she shared with her neighbor. A man who advertised that he sold pet and legal insurance, rarely had clients, and yet inexplicably seemed able to pay his rent.

Despite the room's small size, lack of light, and rather sparse decor, after a year, it had become a comfortable, even welcoming, place for her to work.

She liked her office and she liked the town. Moving so much as kids, she and El hadn't really had what people called a home town. Their dad had retired to Hollis, a small town in Eulalona County, Oregon, because there was a military base where he could take advantage of a VA clinic and other perks.

Within a year their mother announced she'd met

someone and was moving to the East Coast. Once the shock wore off, the three of them had lived together for another year, in a sort of inactive state. Then, Ellen enlisted in the army and a little more than a year later Emma moved to Ashland, known for the Oregon Shakespeare festival and home to Southern Oregon University, where she started college.

Emma had believed her father would stay in Hollis. He'd found a part time job on base and seemed happy enough. He kept busy hunting, fishing and fixing up the house and sometimes went out for drinks with some new friends he'd made. Then a federal cost cutting came along and the base closed. While she was in her second year of college her father, grumbling about politicians and government, packed up and moved to Panama.

The little bit of stability she'd had was gone but Emma was stubborn. She was going to put down roots if it killed her. Why not here? It was just as good a place as anywhere, maybe better.

There was a lot to like about Hollis. Downtown, with its three-story brick and stucco buildings and its colorful awnings was well kept. The business owners and workers she'd met seemed mostly friendly and always willing to chat. It was small town America with a Starbucks on every corner and a solar farm in every other field. A nice combination of new and old. Even the big mural on the side of one of the largest buildings in the center of town seemed to reflect this.

The mural depicted the founders, part of a wagon train climbing a winding trail. At the base it was painted in sepia tones. From there up color was slowly introduced in scenes of fields filled with crops, rivers edged with flowers and a sky so blue it hurt your eyes. Across that sky roared a trio of modern jet fighters that probably represented a fighter wing once assigned to the now defunct base. Honor the old and embrace the new. It was what Emma hoped she could achieve. Remember the past, fondly and without bitterness while being open to change and the future. It didn't sound *that* impossible.

Ignoring her unopened mail, Emma dropped onto her desk chair and took out her phone. It was time to call Gwen and let her know what she'd found, though she hated how little it was.

After she'd filled her in, Gwen said, "But that isn't

really evidence of anything, is it? I mean, those keys could have been dropped by someone coming to look at the place, maybe to buy or lease it. Or maybe one of the firemen dropped them."

"I doubt a fireman could afford the kind of car that key would start, but you have a point," Emma sighed. She hated puzzles she couldn't solve. Though she wasn't ready to give up just yet.

"Should I go ahead and process the claim?" Gwen asked.

"Can you hold off for another couple of weeks? I want to look into a few things. Talk to some of the people in the area." Emma didn't share that the key fob was currently on its way to a lab in Virginia. Special favors, such as the one El had asked from her FBI friend, were best kept secret.

"Sure. That won't be a problem. We need to get more pictures anyway. Processing can take as long as we need, up to a point. If you doubt me, ask anyone who ever put in an insurance claim," Gwen chuckled.

"I have no doubt," Emma said, laughing. "I think that's a pretty well-known fact."

"So, what are these things you're looking into?

What's your next step?" Gwen asked.

Emma was amused by her friend's undisguised interest in a private investigator's work.

"I'm going to ask around the neighborhood to see if there's been any unusual activity around the warehouse lately. That key fob got me thinking that maybe someone was using the place to work on cars."

"You mean like a chop shop?" Gwen asked a little breathlessly.

Emma smiled. "Yes, just like that. Stolen cars, high-end ones, being taken apart for parts. Could explain the keys and the fire. Maybe it was an accident that happened in the process of committing a criminal act. I'm not sure if that would affect your payoff."

"Oh, that would certainly affect things," Gwen said, a happy lilt to her tone.

"I thought it might. I'm also going to drive down to the reservation and talk to the policy holder. Not to harass him or make him think he's a suspect," Emma said, forestalling Gwen's inevitable protest. "I'm just going to tell him I need to clarify that he's the owner of record, blah, blah, blah. You know, just another stickler for process representing the insurance company. If it feels right, I'll ask if he knows of anyone who might have wanted to destroy his property. Who knows, maybe I'll get something, maybe not."

"I don't know. I told you he came across as a pretty sketchy person. He could figure out what you're up to and get angry."

"Have some faith," Emma said. "I can take care of myself."

"Sure, but I'd feel better if you didn't go there alone."

"I'll probably ask El to go."

Gwen's sigh of relief was both obvious and annoying. Everyone always thought that of the two sisters, El was the tough one, that she could handle herself in any situation.

It had always been that way and it wasn't fair. After all, they'd both been army brats, raised on bases across the country and the world. They'd both had the same tough-as-nails father who insisted they learn hand-to-hand combat and have basic gun skills. He wasn't around much, but by damn, his girls would know how to take care of themselves, and they did.

Their shared childhood didn't matter. Her degree in criminal justice and her work as a licensed private investigator didn't matter. None of it compared to El's nine years in the army. First as military police and then as a criminal investigations special agent. Yes, her sister was a certified badass.

Still, she didn't think it was fair that Gwen wanted her to take El along as some sort of bodyguard.

As if reading her thoughts, Gwen repeated herself, "You promise you'll take El with you?"

"I promise I'll ask," said Emma. "Gotta run now."

After she hung up she poured a cup of coffee and was surprised to see her hands shaking. She clenched them around the cup. Forced them to be still. *You're being childish and ridiculous*, she told herself. *Why are you so upset? You know asking your sister for help isn't proof that you can't do the job. It's just smart. So what's with the sibling rivalry? Is that what's getting to you, or is it something else?*

Not wanting to waste time on deep analysis, she sat down and reached for her mail. The phone rang and she picked it up. "Hello?"

"Is this Richland Investigations?"

Embarrassed that she'd answered the phone in such an unprofessional way, Emma stumbled through her answer.

"Yes. Yes. This is Richland Investigations. Sorry."

"Oh, that's okay. We all get distracted. Could I speak to your boss?"

Another spike of shame as she realized the woman on the other end of the line obviously thought she was speaking to some young assistant who didn't know how to answer a phone. She cleared her throat awkwardly and said, "I'm the boss, that is, the owner. This is Emma Richland."

"Oh." Emma cringed at the woman's hesitation, but then she went on. "Well, good. I understand you're a private investigator and that you help people with all sorts of problems."

"Well, that depends. What sort of help do you need?"

"I think someone has been breaking into my apartment. I told the building manager but he doesn't believe me. They won't do anything to stop it."

"Breaking in?" Emma asked. "Breaking in and

taking things? You should call the police."

"No. Nothing is taken. I think he just goes through my things. He tries to make it look like it's the way I left it but it's not. It's very creepy."

"I see. That is creepy," Emma agreed. She picked up a pen and began rolling it between her fingers. "You said he. Do you have an idea who this person is?"

"Only one person has a key to my apartment. The maintenance man. I think it has to be him. Every time I go out grocery shopping or to run errands he must be letting himself in. When I get home I can tell things are different. I can even smell his cheap cologne and the cigars he smokes. I need to catch him so they'll believe I'm not lying. Can you help me?"

"I'd love to help you," said Emma, and she meant it. The idea of someone invading this woman's privacy, rummaging through their things. Oh yes, she'd love catching someone like that. "What was your name?"

"Grace Evers. Would you tell me what you charge."

After she explained her rates Ms. Evers agreed to the terms. Then they set up a day and time, later in the week, when they could meet.

Perfect, a new job and a chance to use the motion

activated hidden camera she'd recently bought. The thing was expensive and now it could start earning its keep. Plus, the case seemed simple. Just a sneaky weirdo to deal with. It would feel great to catch the maintenance man in action and prove her client right.

CHAPTER SEVEN
Monday, September 10

After talking to Grace Evers, Emma got to work, stopping around one o'clock to have some yogurt and a banana for lunch. By then she was sick of paperwork, so she closed up the office and headed for her car.

Twenty minutes later she was on the highway at the south edge of town. She took the last exit and drove into an industrial complex. Turning in she followed a winding road until she reached the back of the lot and a squat brick building. Sunlight flashed off a set of wide double-glass doors. The sign above them, VR Tactical, was easy to spot.

As she pulled in front and parked Emma realized that, since attending the open house nearly a year ago, she hadn't been back to her sister's place of business.

As she thought about it, she wondered if El took her absence as a lack of support or interest. She hoped not. It had nothing to do with El. It was just that although the store had everything a gun buyer might want, Emma already had a gun, and no desire to own more. The shooting range was state of the art, but Emma preferred to shoot at a canyon wall, where the sound echoed off the surrounding hills. She had no desire to fire at a wall, even if it was a full containment bullet trap, stuffed with rubber, in a soundproof room, as her sister had bragged at the open house.

Once inside, she saw glass front cabinets holding handguns, and walls lined with rifles and shotguns. In key positions across the dark gray linoleum floor, display racks held every imaginable accessory, from holsters to safety glasses.

However, the thing that caught her immediate attention was a moose head. It was mounted on the back wall above a door marked "Firing Range" and had definitely not been there the last time. She would have remembered it. It was enormous. Unlike most of the mounted heads Emma had seen, this one looked neither dusty nor molting. Its fur had a sheen to it, the giant curve of antlers seemed polished, and the glass eyes stared down with a sort of majestic tolerance.

"That's Desna," a voice said, and she broke her wide-eyed tourist gaze of the moose head, to look at a man standing behind the counter near the cash register. "Des for short," he said. It's Aleut. I think it means the boss."

"It fits," she said, sparing one more glance at the six-foot-wide antlers and the all-knowing eyes before turning her attention back to him.

A good P.I. would be able to look at someone and describe them in court. That was the excuse she gave herself as she carefully scanned him, noting that he was average in height, maybe a couple inches under six feet with wide shoulders and narrow hips. He wore a black t-shirt with the company logo and it was impossible not to notice how the shirt stretched over those broad shoulders, muscular arms and pronounced abs.

"How can I help you?" he asked, his words echoing slightly. They seemed to be the only ones in the store.

Stepping closer, she guessed he was in his thirties.

His skin was tanned, with small lines at the corners of his eyes that hinted at time spent outdoors. He was close shaven, his hair and eyes dark, nearly black. He had a square jawline, a strong chin, a sort of movie star bad guy look, softened by the dimple in his left cheek when he smiled.

"Is Ellen here?" she asked.

"She's on the range right now, with a couple customers." He checked the bulky black sports watch he wore. "She should be done in ten minutes or so. Is there anything I can help you with?"

"No, that's okay. I'm her sister. I'll just wait for her."

"Oh, it's nice to finally meet you, I'm your sister's partner, Leonys, but everyone calls me Leo."

"What happened to Vargus? I thought he was her partner."

"Ah, that's my last name; only your sister calls me that."

He reached out his hand and taking it, she realized her description hadn't quite captured him. Sure, it was possible to note the white teeth in the friendly grin, but not why it made her respond with a grin of her own. Or why, when their eyes met, it was hard for her to look away. Or how a calloused handshake could stir a response she hadn't felt in a long time. Maybe it was because he was just damn hot. Maybe, it was as simple as that.

He'd been out of the country during the shop's opening, so Emma hadn't met him. In fact, he seemed to travel a lot, at least El had complained about it more than once. Though, to be honest, she hadn't complained that much. After all, the agreement seemed to be that Leo provided the money and El provided the time. Each of them seemed to be living up to their part.

All Emma knew about Leo was that he'd been born in Cuba, that he and El had worked together in the army, and that when he inherited some money, they decided to leave the service and open a business together.

Just then, the door to the firing range opened and El and three men walked into the room. Each carried a range bag with their guns safely zipped inside. The men were in their early twenties, she thought, and were completely focused on El. Emma had to admit her sister looked good. Her hair was held back out of her face by the tinted safety glasses she'd pushed onto her head. She wore hiking boots, khaki green pants, and the same company t-shirt that Leo was wearing. It was just as snug as Leo's and showed off how toned she was.

Seeing Emma, Ellen led the men to the counter and handed Vargus her bag. "Lock it up for me, would you? Vargus will help you with that order," she said to one of the customers, and gave him a bright smile before turning her attention to Emma.

"Hey, what brings you here?" she said. "Finally going to replace that ancient revolver of yours?"

"And have to go to all the trouble of policing my brass when I finally get around to shooting someone? I think not."

"But you could shoot them so much faster," Ellen said, with a phony redneck drawl.

"As appealing as that sounds . . . "Emma let her response trail off. "I have to run out to the reservation. I want to interview the man who took out the policy on the warehouse. He lives there and I was wondering if you wanted to go with me."

Though Emma didn't think she needed help, she'd realized it wouldn't hurt to have company for the long drive.

"I wish I could," Ellen said, "but I have a class coming this afternoon. A group of women who insist on a woman instructor."

"Have they seen Leo?" Emma asked, casting a sidelong glance at him. He stood talking with the trio of younger men who seemed to hang on his every word. Though not the tallest or the toughest looking, he somehow had more of a presence than the others.

"Oh no, you don't," said Ellen softly. "No crushing on my business partner. Mixing business and romance never works."

"It's not *my* business," Emma reminded her sister. "He's not *my* business partner. Also, I'm not crushing on him, or anyone. What does that even mean? What are you watching on television these days?"

"There are stalking laws," Ellen noted, hands on her hips.

"I'm not stalking, I'm admiring," Emma told her sister.

"Well stop admiring. Since I can't go with you, I

was thinking he could go in my place, but only if you keep your hands to yourself."

Emma didn't know what to say at first but then, blushing slightly, said, "I would never. I can control myself. At least for one car ride."

"Oh please. We both know better."

"Besides," said Emma, "I wasn't looking for help, just company."

"I'm sure you don't think you need help, but I know some of the people around there are pretty rough. I'd feel better if he went with you."

Emma sighed. "If he wants to go, fine."

"Hey Vargus," Ellen said, walking up to the counter as the three customers left, a small bell on the door signaling their departure. "Would you mind taking a little road trip with my sister? It would be a great way for you two to get to know each other. She has to talk to someone on the reservation, someone she's investigating, and she could use some back up."

He turned and looked at Emma. She felt his gaze slip across her like fingertips, leaving a warmth she was both drawn to and irritated by.

"I don't really need back up," she told him. "I was

just looking for company. If you have to work . . . Doesn't he have to work?" she said, breaking his glance and looking at Ellen.

"Nope, no regular hours," Ellen said, a note of glee in her tone. "He comes and goes as he pleases. My morning guy called in sick but I have someone coming in this afternoon. She'll watch the store while I'm training. She'll be here in—,"she pulled her phone from her pocket, took a quick look and said—"about half an hour. So, if you want to run down there with her?" Ellen said, looking at Leo.

"I would love to run off somewhere with your sister," he replied, then winked at Emma to show he was kidding.

Neither sister bought it.

"Not run off, you big jerk, run down, as in head south," said Ellen. "The guy she has to see might be some sort of psychotic mouth breathing thug. So of course, since I can't go, the first person I thought of was you."

"How could you not?" he asked, appearing to admire his knuckles.

CHAPTER EIGHT
Monday, September 10

Until recently, Charles "Jelly" Jamison, had been second in command of WIP, which stood for, We Indigenous People. WIP was an organized criminal gang with members from various Native American tribes: Maklak and Yaas from the local area, a Modoc from Klamath, even a white guy who had been adopted and eventually made a blood brother. Skin mattered, sure, and blood mattered, but what WIP really cared about was loyalty, and selling drugs.

Jelly had always been very good at his work, and had believed himself to be a loyal member of WIP, but now questioned if that was true. The half bottle of cheap whisky burning in his gut was not lending any clarity.

He was sitting on an old rusty swing in his cousin's backyard. The sun was warm on his shoulders. A breeze pushed clouds across the blue sky, sweeping them toward the low range of mountains to the west.

Kicking the toe of his boot into the dirt made the swing move a few inches. It creaked in protest.

Behind him the sprawling ranch style house sat empty. His cousins had gone off to a Pow Wow somewhere and he had stopped by to make sure the cattle had water and the dog had food. Both were fine and now he was just sitting, taking slow sips of his cousin's whisky, about as mellow as turpentine, and trying to remember what part of the conversation last week had gotten him to agree to kill his boss, Dodge.

It had been a face-to-face meeting. Murder isn't something you want to plan over the phone. So, they'd decided to meet at Redwing Trailhead. One of the spots along the rails to trails hiking path that ran through town and well beyond. From the trailhead south the path cut through open range grazing land. Between the piles of cow manure and the occasional angry steer it wasn't a big draw to hikers or bicyclists. It was unlikely they'd be seen.

Jelly had arrived early and was sitting on the top of one of the two picnic tables, his feet on the bench seat, leaning forward, forearms resting on his knees. On the outside, a vision of patient waiting, while on the inside his emotions ping ponged from bored to anxious and back again. He was relieved when he finally spotted a dark gray SUV in the distance. Moments later, Beale pulled into the gravel parking lot.

As he watched the tall man get out of his car, Jelly thought that in pressed jeans, white shirt, blazer and cowboy boots Beale looked like a young Kitzhaber, former Governor of Oregon. He was probably less politically ambitious however, seeming content with his job as chief assistant district attorney. Or perhaps it was only that, as the biggest drug importer in the county, it served him to stay out of the limelight. He probably got a big laugh out of seeing the district attorney in the paper or on TV. He played at being a celebrity, while Beale sat in the background and made money like one.

* * *

The Indian moved over and Beale climbed up and sat far enough away so he could half turn and look him in the face. Dodge's Lieutenant, second in command of WIP, wore biker boots, faded jeans, and a red-checked shirt over a blue t-shirt. He had jet black hair, cut military short, a wide face, thin lips, and a nose that looked like it had been flattened a time or two. Of course, that could just be the Indian showing through. He also had brown eyes, shiny and sharp as obsidian. They seemed to pin him in place and examine him, for what he wasn't sure. He broke their gaze first, reaching for a pack of cigarettes in his inner jacket pocket. He held out the pack, "Smoke?"

Jelly shook his head no, so he lit one for himself. Took a long drag. Let it out slowly. "We've got a problem."

Jelly waited, and said nothing.

"I had a meeting with Dodge a couple days ago. He's fucking crazy."

Jelly nodded. "Everyone knows that."

"Well, yeah, but he's getting crazier, like he needs to be locked up crazy."

"How so?"

"We were going to meet at the warehouse, the one WIP bought a few years ago. The one down on Market.

I was late, got held up after work."

"Dodge don't like waiting for people," Jelly said.

"No shit?" Beale took a short nervous draw on his cigarette. "The crazy bastard set the warehouse on fire. When I rolled up the damn thing was nearly engulfed, flames everywhere."

He remembered the scene. The way Dodge stood near the doorway, staring at the fire, a short, barrel chested man, his silhouette made even larger by the bulk of his heavy brown coat. As Beale came up on him, Dodge turned quickly, his twin braids swinging, his lips pulled back in a grin so wide his teeth flashed white. He looked as excited as a kid on Christmas morning.

"What the hell happened?" he'd asked Dodge. Not yet ready to believe he'd started the fire.

"Beauty isn't it? Got bored waiting. Had to find something to do, didn't I? Things in my name. Makes it mine, right? Do what I want with it."

The grin never left his face. Beale should have realized that Dodge wasn't right and shouldn't be messed with, but all he could think of at the moment was the attention the fire could draw. The danger too much attention could put the whole organization in.

"You crazy son-of-a-bitch!" he'd shouted, and he'd put both hands on Dodge's chest and pushed hard. The man didn't budge. Even his smile remained the same. Immediately Beale realized his mistake, but had only enough time to feel an icy ripple along his spine before Dodge reached for him. But instead of the knife or fist he expected, Dodge tore Beale's keys from his hand and threw them deep into the warehouse. Then he laughed.

"What the h-hell?" He'd demanded. His voice, breaking like a little boy's. He'd been so angry he'd even taken a few steps toward the inferno before feeling the intensity of the heat and quickly backing away. "Why the fuck did you do that?" Frustration and rage had driven out his fear of the man, at least momentarily. "What's wrong with you? Didn't you get to rape enough people this week? Damn you. That's not even my car. What the hell, Dodge. What were you think—?"

He turned to where he thought Dodge was standing, his tone already becoming more conciliatory as he realized the rape comment would probably not be taken well. But Dodge was climbing into the black Camaro he'd left nearby. Beale saw the door slam shut as it was moving away. The Camaro's pipes were so loud he could hear them, even over the roaring fire.

The car he had borrowed, and no longer had keys for, was parked two blocks away on the other side of the street. Expecting fire trucks at any moment, Beale knew he had to get the hell out of there before someone recognized him.

Turning in the opposite direction, he walked away quickly, his long strides carrying him to the corner. By then he could hear the sirens. Too many people knew him. He was sweating. Had to get under cover. There was a Dairy Queen on the corner, closed and dark. He headed that way. Behind the restaurant was a trio of dumpsters. He hunkered down behind one and stayed in the shadows as the first truck's lights swept by. The light didn't penetrate the place where he stood hiding.

Once he knew the coast was clear, he slipped out and walked toward downtown. There was a neighborhood bar not too far away. Taking out his phone he searched for a cab company and called them.

They said they'd send a driver to pick him up at the bar in about half an hour. His disheveled look and trembling hands would be mistaken as the effects of too much drinking. No one would connect him to the fire only blocks away.

Shaking off the memory, he came back to the present, and looking at Jelly, said, "Dodge set the fire and destroyed a valuable piece of property for no good reason. Worse than that, there's been more than one time his name has come up at work. Everyone knows he's a rapist. Eventually someone is going to file a complaint. If that happens, I'm betting a lot of women will come forward. That will start an investigation into him and everyone associated with him. We don't want that. Then there's the Padillo thing."

* * *

Jelly stared down at the graffiti-scarred table and offered nothing about the incident, even though he remembered it clearly.

He'd been at Dodge's house, waiting for him. When Dodge got there he'd been so high and drunk that when he tried to sit on the couch he'd slid down the front of it and ended up on the floor. He stayed there, legs sprawled out, head bent forward, his braids nearly touching the floor. Later on he'd told, no he'd bragged, to Jelly about what he'd done.

Jelly was so disturbed by the memory that he couldn't share the whole truth with Beale. He'd never mentioned that Dodge had gone to Miguel Padillo's house and was raping him in front of his children when his wife came home. He didn't share how Miguel had tried to use the distraction to try to get to his gun cabinet, or that Dodge had shot and killed him in front of his family.

He looked at Beale and said, "Dodge told me he caught Ernesto's little brother, Miguel, selling at the high school so he shot him. That could have brought some heat, but I heard you took care of it."

Beale smiled, showing off perfect dental work, "Yeah, it's amazing what a little help from Benjamin Franklin and a promise of future leniency can get you. Practically makes you bulletproof, unless you do something stupid or crazy. Setting the warehouse on fire and killing Miguel were both.

"The way I see it, we only have one option," said

Beale. "Dodge has to go. He's drawing too much attention. Making too many enemies. The Padillo's have been around longer than him. They got a big network and they are pissed. It won't take much for Ernesto to decide to call in some favors and then you know what's going to happen? A war. A war between the Mexicans and the Indians. Is that what you want? Dead people. A whole new group of people running things? I hear the Hell's Angels have been making subtle inquiries, checking the power structure, waiting for an opportunity. Dodge and his crazy bullshit are just what they need."

"What do you want me to do?" asked Jelly, though he already knew the answer.

"I want you to kill him. Why else would I call you all the way out here? I want you to kill that fucking animal and take his place in the organization. I will deal directly with you, and no one but you, so no bullshit competition from inside your organization. I want a smooth transition and no interruptions."

Beale sat back, confident Jelly understood what he was being offered. Reaching down he calmly smoothed the crease in his slacks. "Look, as one businessman to another, last time the town went dry it was bad. I don't want to do that to our customers. We want to keep things rolling. Keep things smooth."

Jelly felt his incisors scrape across his bottom lip and made himself stop. Rose, his wife, said it was his tell when he had a bad poker hand, or bad news to share. This time it was neither of those. This time the hand he was being dealt could be a straight flush. He knew Dodge had been raking in the bucks. He'd bought his tricked-out Camaro with cash. Went to Vegas and Reno whenever the mood hit. Last time he'd dragged Jelly along for company. Top dollar women, top shelf whiskey. Jelly had felt out of place, until he got drunk enough not to care. Then, man oh man.

He felt his teeth dig into his lip again as he thought of those women, two blondes, both tall and beautiful enough to be models. The kind of women from the magazines he used to hide in the back shed. Of course, he hadn't slept with either of them. He was married, and Rose would kill him, no joke, but a blow job wasn't really sex. Damn, that was a good memory.

With the kind of money Dodge pulled in, why he would take Rose along with him, go to Vegas, hell, go to

Hawaii. Fuck the winter. Fuck the snow.

He'd tuned out a bit but tuned back in when he saw Beale was holding out his hand. Jelly reached for it a little awkwardly and the two men shook.

Jelly drug his heels through the dirt under the swing, leaving two furrows in the fine dust. He thought about taking another drink of his cousin's harsh whisky, but the memory of the bad taste kept him from unscrewing the top. The whisky Dodge bought in Vegas that time, now that had been good stuff. Top shelf. Single malt. Expensive though.

That was the way of it. Everything had a price. Just a matter of deciding if you were willing to pay it, that was all. With a sigh, Jelly got up and headed toward the house. He'd return the bottle, lock up, and head home. He much preferred doing to thinking and he'd done enough thinking.

CHAPTER NINE
Monday, September 10

"The reservation is actually three areas," Emma explained as she drove. "One long section along the Diamond River that's about three hundred acres. Plus another two sections of timber, about two hundred acres each. The tribal government is in a little town called Muddy Creek. The man we're driving out there to talk to is Native American, Yaas I think. His name is Dodge Keller. He owns a ranch, or maybe he leases it, I'm not sure about how things work on a reservation.

"He bought the warehouse in Hollis three years ago but he didn't insure it until about a year before it burned. That seemed a little suspicious to Gwen. Plus, the plans he said he had for it likely never went through. When it burned it was pretty much empty except for a few paint cans, and what not. Basically, wasted space.

Emma knew she was over explaining but she didn't know Leo well enough to sit in companionable silence. In fact, there was very little *companionable* about him.

Even though she kept her eyes locked on the road ahead, she couldn't ignore his presence. She certainly couldn't escape the scent of the expensive cologne he wore.

Few of the men she'd known growing up bothered with such things. Her father had smelled like cigars with a side of Old Spice aftershave. Her ex-husband usually smelled like cinnamon. He chewed cinnamon gum constantly. This was no chewing gum. This scent was exotic and masculine, and it made her toes tingle. *Well, maybe not her toes.* Again, a wash of heat rose to her face. She hoped the summer's worth of tan she'd acquired hid her blushing cheeks.

"So, my sister says you're from Cuba. Did you live there long or ... ?"

"Just until I was six. My parents separated and my mother moved my brother and me to the states. First we lived in Florida and then, a couple years later, she remarried and we moved to Maryland."

"We lived in Maryland for a while, when our dad was stationed there," Emma offered, though she knew the shared connection was weak at best.

"Ellen told me," said Leo. "Sounds like there weren't many places you didn't live."

"Yeah, dad's job moved us around a lot."

"Hard on kids."

"Sometimes. What kind of work did you do in the Army?"

"Criminal Investigation, same as your sister."

"Did you start out as an MP too?"

"More or less. I started with a Bachelor of Science in Criminal Justice, then saw a poster and decided to join the army and see the world."

"And did you see the world?"

"Not really, a little bit of Germany and a few places stateside with names that started with Fort."

"Must have been interesting, investigating crimes."

"Later in my career, I guess. In the beginning, I was in protective services and mostly followed generals around all day."

"You mean like a bodyguard?"

"Exactly like a bodyguard. I spent most of my time stuck in conference rooms or on planes traveling from one boring meeting to another. The posters lied," he said, and sighed. It was so exaggerated Emma couldn't help but turn her head to look at him. His obviously phony hang dog expression made her laugh.

"Yes, I can see you suffered. At least you're making up for it now. My sister says you travel a lot. I hope it's not just to go to meetings."

"I try," he said, "and no, no boring meetings. But enough about me. What about you? What made you decide to become a private investigator? You and Ellen both going into law enforcement. Must be a story there. I remember Ellen telling me your dad was in the Army, but not police, right?"

"Right, no police work, that's for sure. He was in communications. When he retired, he was working as a public information officer."

"I see. I guess I figured maybe it was a family tradition. Dads and uncles all cops or something."

"Or moms and aunts?" Emma asked, calling out his sexist remark.

"Yeah, oh damn, I didn't mean—"

"It's okay.

"It's not, but thanks."

There were a few moments of silence. Emma slowed to let a lime green Mustang roar by then said, "Your question made me think about the whole, following in your family's footsteps thing. One of my grandfathers was a logger and the other was a baker. Both grandmothers were homemakers, and my mom was a nurse. I guess I followed her example. I went to nursing school."

"And found out you didn't like it."

"No, I just found a guy I liked more. We got married. He was on the long track to becoming a doctor, so we made a deal. I'd drop out of school and work until he was finished with his residency, then I'd go back to school."

"I'm guessing it didn't work out so well."

"Good guess." Emma was surprised at the bitterness in her voice. Usually she tried to hide her feelings about that too recent chapter of her life, the gut stomp of pain that the memory delivered each and every time. It wasn't bad enough that Mark had cheated on her, but that he'd cheated on her from nearly day one of the six years they were married, and she hadn't had a clue. The fact that she had been so stupidly blind was almost as devastating as his betrayal.

Taking a deep breath, she forced herself to say in a calm and unconcerned tone, "I thought he was having an affair, but he told me I was crazy so often I started to believe him. So, to prove to myself I was wrong I decided to follow him. Turned out I wasn't crazy after all."

"I'm sorry," Leo said.

"Thanks," she said, appreciating the note of sincerity she heard in his voice. "It was the reason I became a PI, and I love it, so I guess it wasn't all bad. Word got around, after I caught him, and a friend told me she suspected her husband was doing the same thing. She wanted me to find out the truth, and I did, her husband was also a cheater.

"That's when I realized I had a talent for following people. I could change my appearance, blend in. My friend gave me a portion of her divorce settlement as a gift. After my divorce I took the money and moved to

Portland and found a job with an investigative service. They didn't pay well but I learned a lot. You need twelve months of work experience to become a licensed investigator in Oregon. As soon as I had them, I took the test and got the license. Then I quit the job, moved back to Hollis and hung out my shingle."

"And the rest, as they say, is history," said Leo.

"I don't know about history. I've barely started," said Emma. "So far most of my work has been finding biological parents or other relatives. Sometimes I work for child services looking for relatives. Kids age out of the foster care system and with no family they end up homeless a lot of the time.

"That's sad."

"It is. It's horrible. But sometimes I get to help people who have been adopted find family."

"Doesn't that ever turn out bad? I mean, do they want to be found? They gave their kid up for a reason."

"Yes, but in my vast experience," she smiled to show she was joking, "I've never had a person say they didn't want to meet their child."

"That's great."

Emma nodded. "It really is. Then there's the less

interesting but steadier work. Fairly often I help people looking for back child support. I also work as a process server for several attorneys, and if the sheriff's office is busy, they contract with me to serve papers on low risk clients. I haven't had a surveillance job in a couple of months. Like I said, steady, but not exactly the most exciting work."

"But overall, you like it, being a PI."

"I do. It's nice to be the boss," she said, verbalizing what she'd been thinking just that morning. There was another reason too, but she didn't share it with him. He might think she was a little strange. One of her favorite parts of the job was the opportunity it gave her to play someone else. To be like an actor and take on a role. She enjoyed the characters she invented so much that she'd even given them names.

There was Barbie, who had a wig of long, straight blonde hair, spidery fake eyelashes, pink lipstick, and dangling earrings. She wore sweaters, a padded bra, tight pants and platform heels.

Then there was Eleanor, who was always ready for a gallery opening with an upswept do, a sleeveless, black dress, ballet slippers and a thin silver cord with a huge diamond around her neck. A subtle statement of her wealth and good taste, as well as a tribute to cubic zirconia.

But Emma's favorite and most frequent persona was Lucy, the iconic soccer mom. She ran around with her hair in a ponytail or a messy bun, a smudge of eyeliner and some gloss her only makeup. She wore black, stretchy leggings, a reversible hoodie, a reversible cap and black Nikes. She could disappear into the shadows like a cat burglar all in black, or transform into an inconspicuous jogger in white shorts, a tank and running shoes.

"I wish I was my own boss," said Leo after a moment. "I know. I know," he said, forestalling her response. "I do own my own business, but it's really your sister who runs the place. As you mentioned, I like to travel. I think your sister wants me to stick around more and teach more classes. Women's self-defense is the big thing right now but I can imagine some student knocking me on my ass. Could I survive such a thing?"

Emma shot another sideways glance at Leo and said. "Is that a fishing expedition? Do you want me to say that is very unlikely, or should I just mention your big muscles?"

"Oh, hell no," he said, sounding truly taken aback. "I'm serious. These things happen. What would become of my machismo if a girl beat me up?"

"Machismo is dead, my friend," she joked. "It died in 1920."

"How come 1920?"

"Because at that moment in US history you no longer had to have a penis to vote."

There was a moment of silence and then, "But what do you use to mark your ballot?"

Emma couldn't suppress a groan. "Oh boy."

"Pretty awful, huh?"

"We should probably find something on the radio."

CHAPTER TEN
Monday, September 10

To reach the address listed on the policy for Dodge Keller they left the highway and drove through Muddy Creek. Leo looked around and said, "This town is so small, I bet their zip code is a fraction. This town is so small, they'd have to widen the roads to paint traffic lines." He paused a moment, then said, "This town is so small, I bet the local Motel 6 sleeps six."

Emma shook her head. "Behave," she told him, though she couldn't help but smile.

Once through town the road climbed, becoming a narrow lane with forest on the driver's side, a sheer cliff on the passenger side. Emma's mouth went dry and the Jeep's engine grumbled as they climbed steadily up the mountain. Emma drove around a wide curve and as they left the canyon behind, she took a deep breath of relief. The land leveled out and she caught glimpses of wide grassy meadows behind the trees lining the road.

After about a mile, Emma spotted the road sign she was looking for and turned off the main road onto a single lane of asphalt marred with potholes. A short distance later the asphalt was replaced by smoother gravel. A fence of barbed wire strands strung between metal posts ran along the right side of the road for a good half mile, and though the road ended at a wide parking area between a large barn and a small house, Emma noticed that the fence continued.

They pulled up to the house and parked beside a newer Camaro, as sleek and black as obsidian. Even the wheels were black. It was so dark and modern that it made a strange contrast to the house, a one story ranch that, over many long years, had rooms added on until it was large and sprawling, with multiple roof lines. The siding was natural cedar, gray with time and weather.

There was also a covered wood deck and a neatly edged flower bed with rows of Iris, their flowers long gone, their long green leaves like blades stuck in the ground.

On the wall between the front door and a picture window someone had hung a trio of the biggest woven baskets Emma had ever seen. Long feathers had been tied to their edges and they lifted and fluttered at the slightest breeze.

Emma was surprised that the house appeared so well maintained. Based on what Gwen had said about the man, she'd expected less care and more chaos.

When they got out of the car, Emma pressed her fists into her lower back and stretched. She saw Leo rolling his shoulders. They were both stiff from the long drive.

The presence of a battered truck near the barn and the car near the house made her think someone was home. She waited a moment. In these rural areas the sound of a strange car usually brought people out to see who'd arrived long before you reached the door. No one appeared.

They walked toward the house and Leo moved past her and climbed the two steps to reach the deck first. It immediately infuriated her, until she recalled he'd been a bodyguard. Putting himself in the way of potential danger was probably second nature. There was no slight intended.

When she reached the doorway, just a step behind, she heard the buzz of flies and caught the smell of decomposition. She exchanged glances with Leo and they both drew their weapons. The door was slightly ajar, Leo used the toe of his boot to nudge it further open. Emma looked past him to peer into the dimly lit room. Before she could make out the shapes, Leo pushed past her and gestured for her to wait. Reluctantly, she did.

After he cleared the house he called to her. Stepping inside, the first thing she noticed was a man's body lying face up on the floor, only there was no face.

Near the body was a dining room table. On it, a tablecloth had been pulled askew, but most remained on the table, held there by the weight of two rifles and a hand gun. Two more guns lay on the floor near the body and had obviously fallen from the table. Under the table she saw a tin which held soiled bits of cloth and with the smell of blood and urine there was another, more familiar smell. Gun cleaning solution.

The dead man she suspected was Dodge Keller, had been cleaning his guns when he'd been shot. There was a sort of morbid irony in that.

Leo had holstered his gun and now she put hers away then took a closer look at the body. The man had worn cowboy boots, jeans and a torn gray t-shirt. Emma swallowed but her throat was dry. She realized she was concentrating too hard on how the room looked, what the man wore. It was a defense mechanism, for she'd seen what the black flies were feasting on, and she couldn't let herself focus on that.

Too late. Turning away, she stepped quickly back outside and onto the deck. For a moment the day seemed to shimmer. She took a slow deep breath through her nose, then blew it out through her mouth quickly. She repeated the relaxation technique three more times. The dizziness passed.

"You don't have to come back in," Leo told her. He was pulling his cell phone out of his pocket.

"I'm okay," she assured him. Steeling herself, she stepped back into the room, careful to avoid the pool of dried blood. It was the reddish-brown color of old liver. Skin, tissue and brain matter were splattered on the floor and walls. Worst was the exposed bone. What remained of the back of the skull reminded her of a shattered china cup.

Emma turned and ran outside, across the deck and down the stairs. Bile rose in her throat. She leaned forward, hand on the fender of her car for support, and threw up.

The retching went on until her stomach was empty, and then some. When the dry heaves finally stopped, she straightened slowly, one arm cradling her aching ribs. She expected to see Leo nearby offering support and was ridiculously grateful that he'd left her alone.

Near the corner of the house was a hose attached to a faucet. She stumbled to it and turned it on, washed her mouth out, gulped some of the water, which tasted like old rubber and heaven. Finally, she cupped her hands under the water, splashed her face and felt better.

As she came around the corner of the house she saw Leo was sitting on the top step of the deck. She walked over and joined him.

As she sat down, Leo said, "Cops are on the way."

She nodded.

"Shotgun, close and personal would be my guess."

"Mine too," she said, closing her eyes for a moment.

"You okay? Pretty brutal in there."

"Probably just something I ate," she said, in a miserably failed attempt to cover up her reaction.

He didn't bother to reply.

They heard the sirens long before the police arrived. Leo even had time to get up and kick gravel over the mess Emma had made in the driveway. She realized that once again he was trying to protect her. An investigator who couldn't handle seeing a dead body would probably not get a lot of respect from the folks in blue.

But maybe she was wrong, still overanalyzing. Her thoughts were a little unfocused. It hadn't been like seeing a dead body on television or even in anatomy class. This was different. The trauma of seeing the dead man was not something she could shake off. Someday she'd have to deal with it, talk to her therapist. For now, all she could do was stand beside Leo and wait for the police.

CHAPTER ELEVEN
Monday, September 10

Emma and Leo were still sitting on the steps of the front deck when they heard tires on gravel and stood up. In the distance they could make out an SUV painted the tell-tale black and white of a police car. It pulled in, the sheriff's department emblem identifying it, partly obscured by a cloud of dust that swirled a bit before settling.

A deputy, wearing a gray on gray uniform got out, gave them a grim stare, and asked, "You the ones who called 911?"

It sounded like an accusation, and for a moment Emma was taken aback. She started to answer, then noticed the deputy, who had given her the barest glance, had all his attention focused on Leo.

"Yes," Leo told him, curtly.

"You say you found a body?"

This time Emma answered. "That's right. In the house. We haven't touched anything but the front door."

"Anyone else here?"

"No," she told him, shaking her head. She looked at his name badge. "No, Deputy Leblanc, we're alone."

"Then let's start with you showing me some identification."

"I'm a private investigator," Emma told him. "My name is Emma Richland, and this is Leo Vargus who is helping me today." She indicated Leo. "My identification is in my car, along with my concealed weapons permit."

"Do you have a gun on you right now?"

"I do," she said, "In a holster at my back."

"Me too," said Leo, "Shoulder holster, left side. I have a permit as well, in my wallet."

"Okay, I need you to put your guns on the deck and take a seat in the back of my car. I need to get the scene locked down."

Emma exchanged looks with Leo, who shrugged

and said, "Sure thing."

Carefully taking their weapons out, they placed them on the deck, then walked to the SUV, climbed into the back seat and shut the door. Effectively locking themselves in.

As Emma watched Leblanc's retreating figure through the holes in the wire mesh barrier between the front and back seats she said, "Well, this is not what I expected."

"Teach us to call the cops," Leo teased. "Don't you know no good deed—"

"I know. Believe me, I know. What's funny is that I work for the Sheriff's Office now and then and I know a lot of the deputies. It would have been nice if one of them had been dispatched. Pretty sure we wouldn't be locked in the backseat of a police car right now. Just my luck."

"Our luck, said Leo. "Lot of the local cops shoot at the range. He's not one I've met before either."

"Okay, *our* luck," said Emma. "Let's plan to stay out of Vegas."

"Agreed." Leo settled back in his seat but after a few moments shifted and then moved again. Emma could tell it wasn't just the stiff seats and the mingled scent of new deodorizer and old vomit that were making him uncomfortable. He looked outside, staring at nothing of note. In profile he was every bit as good looking. His brow was a bit square and his nose had a bump as if it had been broken and healed a little funny. There was a thin scar from the left corner of his lip to his jaw and at least one of his ears had been pierced.

In noticing his imperfections, Emma couldn't help but note the rest. She would have to be careful. There was no denying her attraction to him and she wondered if that was such a good thing. El didn't seem to think so. Now that he had stopped fidgeting, his dark eyes locked somewhere in the middle distance, she felt as if she were sitting beside something coiled and waiting. Something like a cat about to pounce on a mouse, or a lion on a gazelle. What would it be like, she wondered, to be with him.

Motion caught her eye and she looked up to see Deputy Leblanc leave the house and return to the car. He opened the door and said to her, "I'll still need to see your ID but first I have some questions." He took a small notebook from his pocket, and slid a pen from a holder inside. "Do you know the deceased?"

"I don't think so," said Emma. "I came here to speak with a man named Dodge Keller, who lives at this address. Whether or not that's him," she said, gesturing toward the house, "I don't know. I've never met him."

"What were you going to speak to him about?" he asked.

Emma explained that he held the policy on a warehouse that had recently burned down. "I was hired by the insurance company to look into it," she told him. "They want to know if it was arson."

"You were investigating. Trying to prove he burned it down?"

"Or that he didn't. In any case I thought he might have some information that could prove useful. When we got out here the front door was open. When we looked inside, we saw the body and called 911. You got here fast."

"I'm stationed out here and get all the calls for this area," he explained. Looking past her at Leo he said, "Could you give me your driver's license, your gun permit and your phone number?"

Leo recited his driver's license number while reaching into his back pocket to retrieve his wallet. Leblanc jotted down the information, glanced at Leo's cards and returned them.

Then, he said to Emma, "Would you mind getting your identification for me now?"

She nodded and climbed out of the car. Happy to be free. Leblanc shut the door behind her, leaving Leo inside, then escorted her to her car to get her purse. The slow process of making sure they were who they said they were, made the fact that there was a dead body in the house just a few steps away, seem surreal.

Emma's thoughts were interrupted by the sound of sirens as more cars arrived. First another sheriff's car with two deputies who got out and immediately began to unroll yellow tape under Deputy Leblanc's direction. A few moments later the medical examiner's van arrived quickly followed by a plain white car with two detectives from Blue Spruce, the county seat and the town closest to Hollis, which didn't have its own police force.

After introductions, one of the detectives took Leo toward the barn and the other asked Emma to follow him to the far side of the house to answer a few questions. After he learned Emma was a private investigator he said, with a degree of arrogance that immediately made her angry, "Well, you won't be investigating this."

His thick brows were pulled together and his cheeks were bright red, as if he'd just chugged several shots of liquor or his blood pressure was going through the roof. "This is an active crime scene and investigation. *Professionals* in law enforcement will take over from here. PI's aren't allowed to pursue a parallel investigation, so you might as well bill the hours you got. You won't be getting any more."

Thoughts of sharing information with him were immediately torn away. She'd actually had a weak moment when she'd considered mentioning the key fob. Only a tiny moment though. She fully realized that doing so would expose her sister's friend and probably get him and El in trouble. Using the resources of the FBI for side work was definitely a no-no. She'd keep that to herself. In fact, thanks to his attitude, she'd keep everything to herself.

She was not going to put up with being talked

down too, treated as if she were some incompetent amateur. To hell with him. From that moment she decided, if anyone were going to solve this crime, it would be her.

CHAPTER TWELVE
Monday, September 10

After several more questions, most of them directed to Leo, which she thought was a not too subtle demonstration of rampant sexism, they were finally allowed to leave.

There was little conversation between them on the drive back. Both were tired and subdued. Once she dropped Leo off at VR Tactical she headed to her office. She had decided not to tell Leo, or El that she planned to look into the murder of Dodge Keller. El would have a fit. She'd insist on being involved and Emma didn't need or want her or Leo's help.

Gathering her thoughts, she hung up her coat, and ignoring the late hour, started a pot of coffee. Then she sank into her desk chair and grabbed a pen and notepad. What did she know about the murder? The probable name of the victim. Dodge Keller. She wrote it down. Then she noted how she thought he'd been killed, a shotgun blast to the face. That seemed personal, as if someone wanted to erase the man. So maybe someone he'd ticked off?

Emma put the end of the pen between her teeth. What kind of work did Dodge do? According to Gwen he owned a warehouse and planned to rent it. Did he own other rentals? She wrote down the question. That shouldn't be too hard to find out, a call to the county tax assessors. First though, she'd simply Google his name. It was amazing what one could find by just a single online search.

The scent of fresh brewed coffee intruded on her thinking and she got up and poured a cup, added sugar and a couple packets of powdered half and half. About to take a sip she realized the pen was still clenched between her teeth. An old habit. She put it on the desk, took a sip of coffee and made a face. Why didn't coffee ever taste as good as it smelled?

She took the cup to her desk, sank back down into her ergonomically cozy chair and turned on her computer. In the search area of her browser she typed, 'Dodge Keller, Hollis, Eulalona County, Oregon.'

No Facebook or Wikipedia page appeared, which was good. It meant the name was unique enough that there weren't a lot of them. Winnowing through a list of John Smith's would have been tough. Scrolling on she found a reference to John Keller, a hitman in a series by writer Lawrence Block. She should have put more constraints around her search. Maybe on the next round. Ah, the romantic life of a PI.

Scrolling through several more pages she saw Dodge Keller - Hollis CC. When she clicked she found herself on the official page of the Hollis Community College Cougars. The page was a player profile, complete with photo.

Emma stared at the photo of Dodge as a young man. He had skin that looked tan but not especially dark, brown eyes, short dark brown hair. He stared straight into the camera with an amused smile on his face. The only remarkable thing about him was the width of his shoulders.

Emma read his profile. Dodge Keller. Height: 6 foot. Weight: 220. Hometown: Muddy Creek, OR. High

School: Thornbeck High, Hollis, Oregon. Position: Offensive Tackle.

Though Emma wasn't a fan of either playing or watching football, she knew enough to realize that a tackle would have to be both large and fast. She added a note to her list.

Backing out of that page, she continued scrolling until she came to an article from the local Hollis Gazette. In a police log, the name Dodge Keller was highlighted. The entry read: Dodge Keller was arrested on a previous warrant related to the distribution of drugs. He was uncooperative and elected to fight the officer. Police deployed pepper spray as well as a Taser and took Mr. Keller into custody.

Emma noted the arrest then typed 'arrest and Dodge Keller' in the search bar and was rewarded with an additional article showing an arrest for possession and distribution of oxycontin. Keller was sentenced to a year in prison and a fine of $1,000. He was nineteen.

So, the same kid who played football sold oxy on the side and ended up going to prison, got out and kept doing the same thing. Not the best testimony to the efficacy of the criminal justice system. Not a big shock either, but still a little sad. Emma added more notes. She wondered, since he'd been arrested a couple of times, if the police knew him.

Grabbing her cell phone she checked the time, then thumbed through her list of contacts. When she reached John Stiles, a desk sergeant with the Sheriff's Department, she pressed the call button. John was working nights and should be there now. He'd been the first deputy she'd worked with and was the one who contacted her when they needed someone to serve papers. The phone rang only once before he answered.

"Sheriff's office. Stiles here."

"Hey John, it's Emma Richland, how are you?"

"Great, just great. How you been? It's been awhile."

"It has."

"Keeping busy, huh?" he asked.

"Very," she told him.

"That's good, right?"

"Well, it means I can eat and keep the heat on."

John chuckled, his voice hoarse from years of smoking. "According to the weather guesser that's a dang good thing. We got snow in our future. They're saying an early winter."

"Don't tell me that," Emma begged.

"Sorry, no way to stop it. So, what can I do for you? Pretty sure you didn't call for a weather update."

"Nope. I've been working on an arson investigation and somehow it's tied to that murder out on the rez today. You hear about it yet?"

"We did."

He said nothing else and Emma could sense him listening, waiting for her to tell him more. She smiled at the realization that both of them were playing the same game. Be quiet and wait for the other person to fill the silence. She would go first.

"The possible victim, Dodge Keller, was the owner of the warehouse where the arson took place. I was out there trying to talk to him and found the body. I'm the one that called 911."

"No kidding. Have you shared that information, about the arson?" John asked, as expected, a little less friendly and a little more cop.

"Of course," Emma reassured him. "I told the responding officers. I'm calling because I'm hoping you might have heard how the investigation is going."

"Well hell, Emma. The body was only discovered this morning? What sort of miracle are you hoping for?"

"You never know. You guys have a pretty good reputation."

"Still, the ink's not even dry on the incident report."

"No, I get that. Look, Okay, it's not just idle curiosity. I saw the body and it was, well it was disturbing."

There was silence across the line and then, in a gentler voice, John said, "I can imagine. Look all I can tell you is that it's early days, but the buzz around here is that he was likely killed on Sunday morning. The detectives are out there interviewing anyone they can think of."

"Like who?"

"Like anyone who may have seen or heard something."

"You mean anyone in town?"

"I mean anyone seen near the crime scene."

"But it was way out in the country on a ranch."

"Then they'll look for anyone who was driving or biking or walking in or toward that general area."

"That sounds like a lot of work."

"It is. It takes time. Lots of time."

"So, not less than a day," she asked.

"Nope. Not less than a day," he agreed, and she could hear his mood lighten.

"But if, after more than a day, you get some information . . . " She let the question trail off, wondering if the occasional latte and cookie she delivered to his office was about to pay off.

"I guess I was one of the first to get your freshly printed business cards," he said.

"I remember that. It was a big occasion."

"Fine," he said, giving in. "You'll know what I know."

"When you know it?"

"More or less. But you should understand, it's probably not going to be a hell of a lot."

"I'll take what I can get," she said. "Thanks. I'll talk to you soon."

After she hung up, Emma picked up her pen and wrote. Who was in the area this morning and who would know that?

Tapping the pen on the notepad she considered the question. On the way to the Keller house, she and Leo had driven through the small town of Muddy Creek. Living in a small town was a lot like living in a cul-de-sac. Only a few people belonged there so everyone was always attuned to the presence of strangers. If a stranger had come through, someone would have noticed.

She's have to go back to Muddy Creek soon but for the moment she'd stick with working on the computer. There were a couple databases she subscribed too, designed to help people find people. They could be eerily effective.

Pen clenched between her teeth, she settled in for a long night.

CHAPTER THIRTEEN
Monday, September 20

The special phone rang. For a minute Jelly considered letting it go. Let the damn thing buzz and vibrate until hell froze over. Then he thought about Vegas, of Rose in a new dress with her hair done up. He picked it up. "Yes."

"Letting you know there's a pickup today. Eleven this morning. Sharp."

Beale's voice, so smooth and carefully modulated, set Jelly on edge. He scraped his teeth across his lower lip while he wondered why Beale had called him. Usually Beale called Dodge who then let Jelly know.

Maybe this direct call was Beale's way of showing him that Dodge was out. Then a new thought occurred to him. What if Beale figured he'd done as asked and he thought Dodge was already dead? You don't call a dead man.

As if he'd read his mind, Beale said, "Dodge isn't answering his phone."

Jelly heard the question in Beale's voice but said nothing.

"Probably felt rapey and went out looking for some free range pussy," Beale finally offered.

"Yeah, you probably got it right," Jelly told him. Or he's just gone on a drunk and he's passed out somewhere. Jamal driving today?"

"I guess," said Beale."

Jelly imagined he could hear disappointment in the man's voice.

"And yes, Jamal's driving," Beale added.

At least that was something. Jelly had worked with Jamal for a couple years and was about eighty percent sure he wasn't some kind of cop. That was about as sure as he got about anything.

"You should find someone else to do the pickups for you after you take over," Beale suggested. "No more grunt work."

Jelly said nothing.

"Drop it at the usual place," Beale said, though the instruction was unnecessary.

"No problem," said Jelly, trying for a you're-the-boss tone. He didn't like Beale. He never had. Dodge was a bad man, but he never pretended to be anything else. Beale wore a suit, drove a nice car and acted like he earned it all working for justice. He was a bad man pretending to be a good one and that, in Jelly's mind, was worse.

Jelly didn't really want to work for the hypocrite, but taking Dodge's place meant he'd finally be able to give Rose everything she deserved, nice clothes, a new car, a house of their own design.

She'd never quit working, she loved being a nurse, and she'd worked hard to be one. But if they had money they could leave here and she could find a nursing job in a better place. Money gave you options.

He pressed the end call button on the burner phone while visions of floorplans filled his thoughts. Checking the time he saw it was already ten o'clock. Better get moving. He grabbed the keys to Rose's car. He'd driven her to work all week because his piece-of-crap truck was in the shop again. To hell with

American made. To hell with Chevy. Maybe the next car they bought should be a damn Toyota.

As he drove past the only gas station in town, he glanced at the fuel gauge. Three quarters of a tank, no reason to pull in.

Reaching the casino early, he parked in the closest spot he could find and went inside for a cup of coffee and a cinnamon roll. He didn't gamble, thought it was a fool's game, but he couldn't turn down the good food at low prices they used to lure those fools in.

The casino was owned by the local tribes. Neither he nor Rose were members, so they didn't get a cut of the profits. They both joked that they were East Coast Indians, though they'd never been there. The only perk they got from their brown skin was an extra point in their favor when they applied to lease their house, which belonged to the reservation.

Jelly thought the Blue Feather Casino was a hell of a place. A log and stone fortress decorated with life-sized statues of elk and eagles. It held stores and a restaurant and at its heart an enormous gaming room with a high ceiling, and chandeliers that gave out less light than the machines they hung above. A hell of a place all right, with a weird interior design that seemed to worship nature and glitter equally. It was wildly successful.

During the day the restaurant was about half full of old people, either staying in the new hotel wing, which also belonged to the tribes, or in their RV's parked around the perimeter of the parking lot. At night the casino floor was thick with people wagering their pensions and paychecks, and staying half buzzed from the cheap booze that was poured for them like water from an endless source.

He was finishing his second cup of coffee when he heard the hydraulic brakes on a bus. He left money on the table and followed the narrow blue pattern, that wove like a river through the dark green carpet, to the front door. Outside, he leaned against one of the pillars, noticing the sun was heating up the asphalt and mist was rising. The increasing thrum of tires, and the bright glints of light as the sun reflected from chrome, told him traffic on the highway was picking up.

A large silver bus had just pulled into the loading zone. Most of the passengers were disembarking and going directly into the hotel, confident someone would deal with their luggage. They were right, a hotel employee was dragging a baggage cart toward the bus.

One young couple stood beside the storage compartment, waiting for the driver to unlock it and hand them their bags. Once they got their things they too headed inside. A few minutes later, cart loaded, the hotel employee returned to the casino.

In the early days the casino pickup had been more complicated. A porter would take the bag into the hotel and up to a room reserved under a phony name. Jelly would get the bag from there and take it to his car. They soon realized there were more cameras in the casino than outside. Now Jelly took a more direct approach.

He walked up, stood next to the bus and nodded to Jamal. The smell of burning diesel surrounded them. The air shimmered from heat pouring from the exhaust. Jamal wiped his hand across his face, turned to Jelly and said, "Gonna be a hot one. Can I say Indian summer?"

"I can say Indian summer. You cannot," said Jelly, his voice stern but his eyes filled with humor.

Jamal smiled. "I hear you, brother. Got some luggage for you." He reached into the cargo space and pulled out a gray bag on wheels. He set it on the ground and pulled out the retractable handle. "There you go, she's all yours."

Jelly shook his head, pushed the handle back in place, picked the bag up with one hand and did a bicep curl.

"Yep, you're a badass," quipped Jamal. "Bet you could do those all day."

Jelly nodded. "That's why they pay me the big bucks."

"I can see that. You stay safe, huh."

"You too." Jelly said, by way of goodbye.

"Always," said Jamal. Then he bent to lock the storage space as Jelly headed toward the parking lot.

Squinting against the sun, Jelly opened the trunk and tossed the bag inside. He would drive into Hollis, to Hawks Hill, locally known as Snobs Hill. There he'd drop the luggage off at the house of Dr. Denman, a retired dentist, who would cut the heroin with his own proprietary recipe of Tylenol PM and chalk.

The digital radio read 11:23. Jelly decided to make it quick. Dr. D was a talker, but if he hurried he might be able to get away from him in time to have lunch with Rose.

His phone rang. He glanced at the screen. Saw "unknown caller" and answered it.

"Yes?"

The voice of one of his dealers said, "Did you hear? Dodge is dead."

CHAPTER FOURTEEN
Tuesday, September 11

For a moment Emma had considered calling the store and asking if Leo or El would like to go. But the moment passed. Asking for company could too easily be mistaken as asking for help.

Without company, the drive to Muddy Creek seemed to take longer than the last time. At least she felt pretty confident about her next steps. She'd spent hours doing research yesterday. What she was doing now was just another kind of research.

From Hollis, the highway she traveled rolled through scenery thick with lush forests that thinned now and then to reveal the highest peaks of the Cascade Mountain range. Already those not too distant peaks were dusted with snow.

Muddy Creek was small. What was it Leo had said? So small they'd have to widen the road to paint traffic stripes? It truly was small, and not that easy to find if you didn't pay attention.

She kept an eye out for signs of civilization and after a while passed a factory on the right with big smoke stacks releasing puffs of steam that drifted into the sky. There were cars in the parking lot but no sign to indicate what the factory produced. A little further on was a motel fronted by a cafe that advertised berry pies. On the opposite side of the highway was a small airport with a single narrow runway and a single small hanger. On the roof of the hanger someone had painted a big red arrow and the words, Muddy Creek.

Emma slowed and turned off the highway, drove past the airport, over a narrow two lane bridge across a small river and onto Main Street. The street seemed to live up to its name and took her through the center of town, past small homes, a church, a grocery store, a post office, another church, a tribal office and a community center.

There were only a few people in sight. She saw a young mother holding her son's hand and preparing to cross the street. There were two old men sitting on a bench outside a barber shop. They had gray hair, one cut short, one in long braids. The braids were the only thing she'd noticed that said Native American. Otherwise the little town on the reservation could have been anywhere.

She noticed a Chevron station on her right. The only building beyond it had boarded windows and a large faded sign that read, "Muddy Creek Second Hand." The road divided there, the left fork following the base of a hill back around the town, the right going up a hill and disappearing behind a forest of pines and firs. It was this road she and Leo had taken to Keller's house just yesterday. It was strange to think they'd found the body only a few hours ago.

Emma pulled into the gas station, past the pumps and into a parking spot in front of the empty store. The building had a cedar facade like an old western saloon, with a big picture window papered with old flyers and advertisements for lost dogs, cars for sale, babysitting services. The usual.

As she entered, a bell chimed and a woman she judged to be in her late fifties, with blue eyes and sun damaged skin, looked up from behind the counter and smiled.

Despite the lines that crisscrossed her face she was attractive. Her thick gray hair was swept into a tidy bun. She wore heavy turquoise jewelry, a squash blossom necklace and earrings, and silver and turquoise rings on each finger. She wore a blue button down shirt and black jeans. Emma knew, without looking, that she'd be wearing worn cowboy boots. She looked like a retired rodeo queen from somewhere in the Southwest.

"Anything I can help you with, hon?" The woman asked. Emma noticed she wore a name tag that read, Audie and wondered if she'd been named after the car, or the fifties era cowboy actor. Her dad had tried to get Emma to watch the old black and white films but she'd never been interested.

Emma couldn't help but smile at the unexpected friendliness of her tone, even if it was just well rehearsed customer service. She took out her license and placed it on the counter. Audie looked down at it and her smile didn't waver, she just raised one questioning brow.

"I'm a private investigator," Emma said. "I'm looking into a murder that—"

"Dodge," the woman said, nodding. "You're looking into Dodge Keller getting shot. I heard all about it when the cops came in asking questions last night."

"So, the police have already spoken to you. Did you know Dodge?"

"Know him? Not really. Know about him? Some. I mostly sold him gas and cigarettes. I've only worked here for three months, but you know, small places, you get to know everyone pretty quick, if not directly then through gossip someone is bound to share."

"And what kind of gossip did someone share about Dodge?" Emma asked.

"Just that he wasn't to be messed with, especially if he was drinking. I'm used to that though, a lot of folks get mean when they drink. Boss told me Dodge was known to have a violent streak that got worse after his mamma passed. He never gave me any trouble though. Just paid for what he wanted and went. Not a big talker, but that's okay. I can talk enough for two."

"Were you working Sunday morning?"

"I sure was. I'm the new person after all."

"Did you see many people that morning? I'd especially like to know if you saw anyone driving up Main, heading east.

"You mean up to Dodge's place? That's the same question the cops asked so that's an easy one. I've already thought it through. There were four people I remember seeing that morning. There was Norma Mackie, Willy Keene, Rose something. I don't know her last name. She's married to a guy named Jelly, which is a name that you don't forget, right? You gotta wonder where that name came from. I mean, was he born with it or—"

"That is an unusual name," Emma said, cutting off the self-professed talker. "You said there were four people you saw that morning?"

"Right. The fourth was Harry. He's a sheep farmer who lives right up that road. The turnoff is past the Mackie place on the left if you're heading up that way. Not sure about his last name either, but I think it's Allstaff or Olsen. One of those Norwegian names. Lot of Norwegian farmers settled in Oregon, or so I hear."

"Thank you, this is really helpful," Emma said, "Do

you have something I can write on? I should put those names down before I forget them."

Audie pushed the feed button and tore off a length of register paper handing it and a pen, adorned with a giant plastic Easter lily, to Emma.

"Thanks," Emma said again, quickly jotting down what she'd learned.

"You're welcome," said Audie. "Thing is, I don't believe it was one of the folks I saw driving who killed him. Who the hell would be dumb enough to drive through town if they planned to kill someone? They'd have to know they'd be seen."

"Yeah, that makes sense, but how would someone get to Dodge's place without being seen?"

"Well, me and a few of the folks who have lived here awhile talked about it and we agreed. If it was us we'd cut around town on a horse or on foot. We think whoever killed Dodge probably parked within walking distance and hid their car up some old logging road.

"From what I was told, the best thing would be to park up near Jansen's Mill, walk along Deer Bone Ridge, low enough I'd be in the tree line, then hike down to the house. All you'd have to do to get out is od it all again only this time in reverse. Makes a sort of sense, don't it?"

"That's pretty specific. You think it has to be someone familiar with the area?"

"Makes sense doesn't it?"

"I guess," said Emma.

"Lot of it's just talk though," said Audie. "I'd bet they don't get a lot of murders out here. I imagine the whole town will be talking about this awhile. You still plan to talk to the people I saw that morning?"

Emma nodded and decided it was time to go.

Audie had put a lot of thought into how she would have murdered Dodge. Did she know Dodge better than she claimed? Should she be added to Emma's list of suspects? Maybe there was more to her than a friendly smile.

CHAPTER FIFTEEN
Tuesday, September 11

In addition to the names she gave her, Audie had given her directions to some of their homes. After paying for a diet coke and a fill up, which seemed only fair, Emma headed to the Mackie place.

Tonya Mackie was a widow who ran a huge hay operation along the Mackie River. Named after one of her husband's ancestors no doubt. Audie had told her the Mackie place was on the same road she'd taken to get to Dodge Keller's yesterday.

How had she passed by it without noticing? The entrance was hard to miss. A huge sign loomed above it with the words Mackie River Ranch burned deep into the wooden cross piece. She wondered if Leo had seen it. Had he been as preoccupied as she'd been? It was nice to believe he'd been as distracted by her presence as she'd been by his. Shaking her head, she pushed away the thought.

From the entrance, the house was another quarter mile away, all of it across Mackie land. Emma's Jeep shook as she drove across a cattle guard a little too fast. At first barbed wire fences lined the road, but as she slowed to drive across a second cattle guard, she saw that the fence ended. She found herself driving past scattered groups of cows who grazed on stubby grass and eyed her with frank speculation. There was nothing between her and the cows and it was a surprisingly scary feeling. Cows were large.

"Moo," she said to them in an effort to show them she was a friend. Though of course, she was not. She was hungry and all she could think of was grabbing a burger on the way back to town. She hoped cows weren't mind readers. She'd never make it out alive.

The house was a single story, as deep as it was wide. It was painted white, with white trim and had a green metal roof. To the right of it a long building with the same green and white theme held a row of farm equipment. What the row of convoluted metal on wheels were used for was a complete mystery to Emma.

Smoke was rising from a chimney and Emma parked next to a mud-spattered Jeep and walked up to the house. As she stepped onto the front deck she could hear dogs barking inside. She knocked and the door opened immediately, the woman who answered her knock had undoubtedly been alerted by the dogs the minute Emma pulled into the driveway.

Two small border collies wound around their owner's feet like fuzzy slippers. The woman who stood there was short and stooped. She appeared to be in her seventies or older. One age-spotted hand clutched the handle of a cane. Her tightly permed hair was dyed an improbable dark brown and she'd applied blush, two irregular red blotches on her cheeks. "What can I do for you?" she asked with a welcoming smile. "Are you lost?"

"Not if you're Mrs. Mackie."

"I am," she said, her look growing more suspicious now that her theory had been disproved. Emma realized that the few strangers this woman saw at her door were most likely lost. She probably didn't see a lot of door-to-door salesman way out here. Not when the doors were so far apart. Maybe that was why the woman hadn't asked who it was before opening the door. It seemed foolish to Emma. Was she a trusting soul, or just too tough to be scared?

Emma gave Mrs. Mackie a smile and said, "I'm a private investigator, looking into the death of your neighbor, Dodge Keller. Do you have time to talk?"

"I do. Not sure what I can tell you though."

Emma noticed the woman wasn't inviting her in. Maybe she wasn't that foolish after all. "You were seen driving through town yesterday morning, a little before the time the ME says Dodge was killed."

"Oh my. Does that make me a suspect?" she asked, an unmistakable twinkle of amusement lighting up her eyes.

"No, I don't think so," Emma replied. "At least you're not on my list—yet." She let the last word sit there a moment and was rewarded with a smile. "I was wondering if you saw anyone driving toward Dodge's house around that time?"

Mrs. Mackie, nodded. "Well yes, as I told the police, I did see someone that morning. I saw Willy Keene. I told them I thought he'd probably get a ticket if he doesn't get some work done on that truck. He's dangerous in that old thing. I think the steering is bad. He was bouncing all over the road.

"His father could buy him something better. Got money falling out of his pockets. Though you'd never believe it to see him, or the way he keeps his family. The Keene's aren't too keen on spending money." She chuckled at her play on words and Emma couldn't help but appreciate the woman's upbeat personality.

"I remember that morning," she continued, "because I went off to have breakfast with my daughter at the Copper Kettle in Hollis. Then I went and got my hair done. It was getting too long, wouldn't hold a curl."

"It looks great. Do you like your hairdresser?" Emma asked. "I haven't found anyone I like."

"Oh my, yes. Her name is Kylie Lynn," Mrs. Mackie offered, with a wide smile. "I just love her. She works out of the Crystal Palace Salon on Evergreen. You'll want to call first to make sure you get her."

"I'll do that," Emma promised.

"Would you care for a cup of coffee?"

"Thanks, but I'm in a hurry. So, you're positive. That morning you didn't see anyone but Willy Keene. No one walking, or riding a horse?

"Only the Keene boy's truck." she repeated.

After thanking her, Emma left. The woman was nice, maybe a little lonely, and Emma was pretty sure she'd told her all she knew. Her next stop was just a little farther up the road. A mobile home that belonged to a woman named Rose.

The double wide sat on a couple of acres. Emma conjectured it either belonged to the Mackie Ranch, or once had, and had been split off and sold. To the left of the house was an orchard, to the right a garden. It had been harvested and tilled and now sat waiting for spring planting. The house was painted a cheerful yellow with white trim. The wood deck was painted white and white lattice skirted it. Emma climbed the stairs, enjoying the bright yellow and orange mums in clay pots that had been placed on the ends of each step.

In the center of the door, at eye level, a decal had been affixed, the silhouette of a flying eagle with the word NATIVE spelled out beneath in large capital letters. Emma knocked and waited.

There was no response to her knock but she wasn't surprised. There had been no cars in the driveway or the carport. As she was turning to leave, she heard tires on gravel and watched a blue sedan pull into the driveway. She felt awkward, as if she'd been caught at something. Pushing the guilty feeling away, she put on her friendliest smile and walked to the edge of the deck.

The woman who got out of the car looked Native American to Emma, though she realized that was probably location bias at work. In a different setting she might have looked Italian or Spanish. She had jet black hair twisted into a thick bun, a wide face, and big brown eyes that stared directly into Emma's. The teal scrubs, gray sweater and comfortable looking white sneakers she wore shouted health care professional to Emma. Over one shoulder she carried a leather purse stamped with western designs. In her hands she held a bag of fast food and a drink in a large to-go cup.

"Can I help you?" the woman asked in a firm tone that sounded practiced and professional. The kind of tone you'd expect from someone telling you it was time to take a pill or have your bandage changed.

"Hi," Emma said, still feeling awkward. "I hope so. Are you Rose?"

"That depends," the woman said, a soft smile changing her suspicious look to a friendlier one. "What are you selling?"

"Nothing. I promise," Emma said, and this time her smile was genuine. "I'm a private investigator. I'm here following up on a shooting that happened yesterday morning."

"You mean Dodge Keller?" the woman asked.

"Yes," said Emma.

"But why would you want to talk to me?" she asked, looking puzzled.

"You are Rose, right?"

"Yes, Rose Jamison. Now, what is this about?"

"You were seen driving through town yesterday morning, in the direction of the Keller house. Haven't the police questioned you?"

"They haven't." She climbed the steps and moved past Emma toward the front door, juggling the purse, the paper bag, the soda, and a set of keys.

"Here, let me help you," Emma offered.

Rose handed her the soda, unlocked the door and with only a moment of hesitation, went in then gestured for Emma to follow.

The inside of the house was as tidy as the yard indicated it might be. A leather couch and chair faced a wood burning stove on a river rock hearth. The painted skull of a buffalo hung near it and a few good pieces of art featuring Native American scenes graced the rest of the walls.

Beyond the living room, was a dining table, empty but for a woven basket filled with dried flowers. Rose put her lunch on the table and hung her purse from one of the ladder-back chairs. Emma put the soda down next to the paper bag.

"Please, take a seat," Rose said. Emma sat down in a chair diagonal to hers.

"So, you want to ask me why my car was seen yesterday?" Rose frowned, reached into the paper bag, removed a straw, unwrapped it, poked it through the plastic lid and took a sip of soda. Finally she said, "My car is seen in town every day. I live here."

Emma noticed her initial friendly manner was fading fast. She said, "Yes, and I didn't mean to make you think you were a suspect. I'm surprised the police haven't talked to you. They, and I, want to know if you saw anyone else. Especially anyone driving past your house toward the Keller place."

"I see, and I understand why the cops would care, but how about you? Who are you working for?"

Emma said, "I'm working for an insurance company. Dodge Keller had a policy on a warehouse that burned down. Now he's been killed. I'm curious if those two things are related. Did you know him?"

"Let me see your identification?"

Emma dragged it from her purse and, after a thorough examination, Rose nodded.

Emma was increasingly aware of the smell of burgers, especially since she'd been craving one since seeing the Mackie's cows. Rose's lunch was getting cold. "I'm sorry I caught you at lunch," she said.

"I'm surprised you caught me at all. I rarely come home for lunch, it's a bit of a haul. I work the early shift at the hospital. Took a two hour lunch so I could run some errands. Had to take the car in for an oil change and then hit the DMV to renew my registration. It's all about the cars, right? Anyway, it took less time than I thought so I grabbed some fast food and came home."

Emma's gut, as Gwen liked to call it, went on alert. Rose hadn't struck her as chatty, yet suddenly she was over explaining. Was she nervous about something?"

"So, did you know Mr. Keller?"

"Not really. I mean, he and my husband hung out sometimes, got a beer after work, that sort of thing, but I didn't really know him."

"Maybe I should speak with your husband then." suggested Emma. She almost said Jelly but wasn't sure Audie hadn't made a mistake. She said she'd only had the job three months. Maybe she'd misheard.

"You can't. He's out of town."

"I see, and what's his name?"

"Charles, though really he won't know anything about this. He's on a job. He does construction. He'll be gone for a month or so."

"Oh, well maybe you can call him for me. I'd like you to ask him whether he knows of anyone who was angry with Mr. Keller. If he knows of anyone who would have wanted to burn down his building, or wanted him dead. If you prefer, I can give you my number and you could ask him to call me. I'd like to find out if Mr. Keller was worried about anything or anyone."

Rose chuckled.

Emma gave her a quizzical look.

"You didn't know Dodge, that's for sure. The man didn't have the capacity for worry. I mean, like I said, I didn't know him well but I've heard he liked to fight. In fact . . ." She paused. Ellen could almost see warning lights go off as the woman looked down, picked up the straw wrapper and began folding it. "In fact, he had a bad reputation," she continued, "but he never did anything to me or my husband. They weren't all that close though. Like I said, just the occasional drink."

Emma wondered at the abrupt shift. Was Rose simply concerned that she sounded like a gossip or was she hiding something? She made a mental note to remember this later.

"I'll let you get back to lunch. I just have one more question for you. Did you see anyone else yesterday morning? Any cars that might have been heading in the direction of Dodge's house? Anyone walking?"

"No, I'm sorry. When I left it was dark and no one was out. It's like a ghost town that early in the morning. I don't remember seeing a car, or anyone, until I hit the highway."

Emma apologized for her timing and for letting Rose's lunch get cold.

"That's okay, I'll just nuke it," she said.

Emma thought, from the way she wrinkled her nose at the mention of lunch, that Rose had probably lost her appetite. She imagined the bag hitting the garbage can as soon as she left. She just wasn't sure why. There had definitely been something off in their conversation. Her gut was sure of it. Her brain just hadn't caught up yet.

She drove to the sheep rancher's next. As Audie had said, his place was a quarter mile further up and on the opposite side of the road from the Mackie Ranch. Like the Mackie's, the house was off the main road at the end of a gravel road that wound through trees and then through open grazing land.

This time, instead of cows, herds of sheep moved slowly through the scenery, grazing at the brown stubble or sleeping, their forms reminding Emma of ragged balls of dirty lint.

Part of the house was one story, part was two. Emma guessed the single story had been the original cabin and the rest had been later additions. It was painted white on white like the Mackie place but had a red metal roof instead of green. A wood and wire fence surrounded the house, probably to keep out the sheep. Emma parked outside, opened the unlocked gate and walked in.

A dog appeared from behind the house. She hesitated a moment, her hand still on the gate, but the dog only trotted up, sniffed at her ankles and turned, as if to lead her to the house. The image of a perfect butler.

A sign beside the door read, 'Welcome to the Olstad's.' At least she now had the correct last name. She knocked and rang the bell but there was no answer.

To the left of the driveway a large carport held an old station wagon with wood panels and an RV. The stall nearest the house was empty. The tracks leading to it were worn the deepest. She suspected the vehicle he drove most often was missing and that Harry Olstad was not home.

She took out an index card, wrote a short note asking him to call, added a business card, then slipped both between the screen door and the door jamb.

The last person on her list was Willy Keene. Unfortunately the only thing Audie could tell her about him was that he didn't live in Muddy Creek. Not sure what step to take next, she decided to listen to her growling stomach, find a restaurant, and give it some thought.

CHAPTER SIXTEEN
Thursday, September 13

The Major Crimes Unit met in the main conference room of the Eulalona County DA's office in Blue Spruce, the county seat. It was every bit as nice as the Board of County Commissioner's work room. A fact the DA had pointed out on more than one occasion. He wouldn't be doing that today though. He was in Eugene for the morning at a tri-county meeting where, if they'd set it up right, he'd drink a little scotch and play a lot of golf.

Beale, as Chief ADA, would represent the DA's office today. He took his seat, a leatherette swivel chair pulled up to a long rectangular table. The table was dark wood with darker lines of inlay. As any hobbyist woodworker would, he admired it, running his hand across the surface almost affectionately.

As he sat there, the room began to fill. The county sheriff and some of his deputies arrived, followed closely by delegates from most of the city police departments. The last to arrive was the station commander from the state police.

Beale looked around. He knew most of the people there but there were some new faces as well, new cops. He barely suppressed a grin when he spotted those fresh faces. New cops were always hungry to make their bones. Perfect.

One of the admin assistants fluttered around pouring coffee, setting out pitchers of water and a couple boxes of donuts. Discreetly, he checked out her ass. Some of the guys bitched about the change in dress code. Few of the women wore dresses anymore, but Beale didn't mind. Tight slacks over a tight ass beat bare ankles any day.

Bernie Zhang, Chief of Police of Blue Spruce, was talking. Something about a drug deal gone bad. Everyone thought Dodge Keller had been killed over drugs. That maybe someone had taken his stash and then shot him. Beale took his attention off the admin and refocused on the meeting.

"We all know the guy had a lot of enemies," said one of the Hollis City cops.

Beale couldn't remember his name and would have to make a point of finding out. Hard to be the friendly guy at the DA's office, the counterpoint to the serious guy, if you couldn't recite their names, the names of their wives, their kids, and their fucking dogs.

"I heard he had a reputation for raping women," said Leblanc, the deputy who had been the first responder.

"He did," said one of the new deputy DA's from Beale's office. "Everyone figured as soon as one of them came forward we'd have him. Get one to talk and it usually gives others the courage to come forward. Once that happens, it's a pretty easy conviction." The man looked toward Beale as if seeking confirmation. Magnanimously, Beale nodded.

The conversation drifted. Moving away from the issue at hand, the murder of Dodge Keller, to other, less interesting cases. Beale stifled a yawn and told himself to be patient. He needed the conversation to go in a certain direction, but he didn't want to steer too much. He was confident that if he just waited, an opportunity would present itself. Always let them think it was their idea. Management 101.

Finally they came back to the day of the murder. The lead detective gave a summary of what they'd found at the Keller residence. Then he said, "We talked to a local and learned four individuals had been seen either heading to or from the direction of the Keller residence that morning." Consulting his notes he recited, "Rose Jamison, Harry Olstad, Norma Mackie and Willy Keene."

When he said the last name Beale gave out a small sound, a sort of whistle between his teeth. Those seated near him shot him a quick look. He rubbed the back of his neck and gave a chagrined smile.

The detective, who hadn't noticed, went on. "We got confirmation on the presence of two of them from a worker at the community center. A guy who had gone in early to set up for an event. Those two are Harry Olstad and Willy Keene. We've spoken to one of them, Mrs. Mackie, and are setting up interviews with Keene and the other two.

Two recently hired cops from Blue Spruce were sitting next to each other, directly across from Beale. One had a thin face, dimpled chin and wore an intent look, like every word had to be memorized.

The other was all muscles, biceps stretching the fabric of his shirt, with a bullet head he'd shaved nearly bald. Beale leaned forward just a little and in a low voice asked, "Is this Willy guy as bad as everyone says?"

The deputies exchanged a look. Two new guys trying to fit in and eager to give the right answer. Muscles turned back first. Nodded sagely.

Near the end of the meeting when they'd finished the agenda and the conversation was less structured, Muscles, Officer McVay, according to his name tag, finally found his chance to fill Beale in. He leaned forward and confided, "Willy Keene will be the hardest suspect to interview."

Beale nearly smiled. It was just the opening he'd hoped for. Giving McVay his full attention, he nodded his approval. "Yes, I agree. We all know what a bad character he is. The DA's office wants him, but we don't want any of you taking unnecessary risks. We know he's armed and dangerous and that he's not going to quietly let himself be arrested."

"We'll be ready for him," McVay said.

Beale wore his most concerned expression. "I'm not sure you can ever be ready for someone that dangerous."

"I've run into him before," shared Deputy Leblanc, joining the conversation. "You know, out there in Muddy Creek. He's got a bad reputation all right. Thinks he's tough."

Everyone, including Beale was giving LeBlanc their full attention and he loved it. Hell, Beale thought, if the kid were a dog he'd be wagging his tail.

"Willy Keene's a badass," Leblanc warned the two young officers. You need be careful."

Beale nodded gravely, letting his concern for them show, while on the inside he was smirking. It was almost too easy. Ducks in a barrel. Everything was going as planned and he deserved to be pleased with himself. The only hard part was not letting it show.

After the meeting, Beale went to his office, closed the door and took out his burner phone. He bought one every couple of months, like clockwork, and though he knew it was probably paranoid, he did it anyway.

"Hey," he said when Jelly answered. "I got the boys in blue wound up. You think you can track down that kid?"

Jelly frowned. "Not much to track. I know what he drives. I know where he lives. Know where his father lives. He's going to show up at one of those places."

"Not if he hears we're looking for him. Kid like that will run."

"Maybe. Would that be a bad thing?"

"Not necessarily, but the case would stay open, so not the best outcome for us."

"Still, the kid didn't do it. Seems wrong to set him up for this."

"Look, kid's got a juvenile record for assault. His type, well he's bound to do something, if he hasn't already, that will eventually get him locked up. Besides, I'm betting on him and a smart lawyer to come up with a defense. Maybe the kid had to protect himself from Dodge. Maybe he had to shoot Dodge to save his own life. There were enough guns in the place. Kid's young and Dodge had a bad reputation. At best he'll get manslaughter and we'll recommend a light sentence. In fact, I'll see to it."

Beale had no intention of telling Jelly that the last thing he wanted was for the Keene kid to appear in court. He'd started to talk to Jelly about it on an earlier phone call and immediately felt the push back. Jelly might have been able to take care of Dodge, but something about setting up the kid bothered him. You just never knew about people. He'd have to think some more about Jelly running WIP. Jelly. What a dumbass name.

Promising to find the kid and let Beale know where he was, Jelly hung up. He'd been outside, raking leaves against the base of a row of roses they had planted along one side of the house. The extra insulation should keep them alive over the approaching winter. It worked last year. Two years, he mused, since he and Rose had rented the house. Two years in the same place. It was nothing short of a miracle.

From the time they'd run away from the foster home where they'd met, they'd taken work wherever they could find it. For a few years they'd followed the harvest, working on farms, Rose taking whatever classes she could find. When he realized the constant moving and lack of funds was killing her dream of using her degree to start a career, Jelly had accepted a job from Dodge. He promised Rose he'd find a real job as soon as he could. In the meanwhile he took whatever handyman work he could find and made deliveries for Dodge.

It was stability of a sort, but he'd never expected it to last. At first Jelly had even discouraged Rose from planting flowers or trying to grow a vegetable garden. He didn't figure they'd be around long enough to see the flowers or harvest the food.

She'd smiled and ignored him, digging the soil, planting the seed. Ever hopeful of a place to call home, Rose always planned for the future. Expecting change and chaos, Jelly never did. Maybe that's why they were so happy together. Their differences creating a sort of balance.

As if she'd been summoned by his thoughts, Rose appeared from the back of the house. In her hands she carried steaming cups.

"Hot cocoa." she said.

"A little early for this isn't it?"

"I think we'll get snow soon," she said, looking up at the cloudless blue sky.

"Does this prediction come from your Shawnee intuition?" he asked playfully.

"No, it comes from the weather guy on KTMT," she said.

He noticed her long hair was braided. One thick braid that hung down to her waist. He wanted to reach out and give it a tug. She couldn't punch him while holding two cups of cocoa. The intention must have shown in his eyes. She shook her head. "No you don't. Your hands are gross."

His hands were pretty grimy from yard work. That was true. He looked at them, looked at the braid again.

"I'm warning you," she said. Then she held out one of the cups of cocoa, slowly tilted it.

"Okay. Okay. I'll be good."

"You promise?"

"Yes. Damn woman." He took the cup she offered. Caught the scent of rich hot chocolate.

"Who was that?" she asked, pointing her chin at the phone he still held.

He tucked it in his back pocket. "Beale."

"I don't like him."

"I know."

"I didn't like Dodge either."

"I know that too."

"We should leave here."

"No."

"Why? You were ready to go before. After Beale asked you—"

"Asked me to kill someone? You know I couldn't do that but after he called to congratulate me for a job well done. What was I supposed to do? It was like, I don't know, like a miracle or a lucky break. It meant I didn't actually have to kill Dodge and we could stay. Look," he said, indicating the row of thorny bushes. "I just tucked your roses in for the winter."

"We can dig them up. Take them with us."

"Ground's too hard."

"Harder than your head?"

Jelly sighed.

"That woman who came around yesterday looking into that fire. I'm sure she wants more than just whether I saw someone. I'm worried," admitted Rose.

"I told you. I didn't kill Dodge. I just let Beale think I did."

"I know, and I believe you, but that woman. I told her a stupid lie. I told her you were out of town for a month. It won't take her long to figure out that's not true. She'll wonder why I made it up. What was I trying to hide? I should have said nothing or told her to go away."

"It will be fine," he reassured her. Putting one arm around her waist, he gently pulled her against his side. "I'll stick it out one more year. I wanted to make a ton of money and give you everything in the world. But ever since Beale asked me to kill Dodge, the more I've thought about it, the more I've realized what a fool I was to work for him. We'll put away every penny we can and then we'll go. Just one more year, I promise. I don't want to start somewhere new with nothing. Not ever again. You deserve better."

"Oh please," she said, putting her free arm around him. "I barely deserve you."

"I never thought you'd admit it. You really are crazy about me."

"No, I'm just plain crazy."

"That works for me," he told her. "You know, as long as we stay together we'll be fine. You believe me?" he asked, giving her a squeeze.

"I believe you," she said. But she was thinking of that investigator, the way her eyes had looked into hers, the way she'd watched everything. A chill ran down her spine that had nothing to do with the cooling weather.

CHAPTER SEVENTEEN
Thursday, September 13

After leaving the scene of Dodge's murder, Willy had run home long enough to throw some gear together, then set up camp at the old fire lookout. The lookout, which once sat on stilts, had fallen over, leaving a decaying pile of timber behind. For years Willy's father had used it as a deer blind and primitive shelter, fashioning a small but usable area under the edge of what was left of the roof. It provided some protection from the weather and there was even a fire pit in one corner with a vent hole so you wouldn't choke to death while trying to stay warm.

Maybe being there reminded him too much of his father. Got Willy to thinking about him and wondering what advice he'd have for his only son. Or maybe it was just that he got bored. In any case, after a few days he packed up his camping gear and drove to his childhood home. Now he sat on his dad's front porch, in one of two rocking chairs. His dad sat slowly rocking in the other.

For the first time Willy noticed the age spots on the back of his father's hands. How had he not noticed before? Maybe because they just hadn't seen that much of each other in the past couple of years. Not since he'd moved out.

Willy had saved up and bought a piece of land with an old cabin on it, basically a shed kit but someone had insulated it and added a fireplace. The property it sat on was only a quarter acre, small by local standards. However, the development the lot was part of had gone bankrupt, so the cabin sat in the woods, surrounded by nothing but dozens of empty unsold lots.

Alone in the middle of nearly a hundred acres, there was no one to complain about the hodgepodge of sheds and fluttering white canopies where Willy housed his trade goods. Those goods included appliances of all kinds, motorcycle and car parts, small boats, bicycles, tools and whatever he thought someone, somewhere, sometime, might want.

In one of the sheds he'd rigged grow lights and sown a small crop of marijuana, which helped with the bottom line. Willy figured he was never going to be rich in money anyway, but he did what he wanted, when he wanted, and he got by.

Willy's dad's house wasn't as isolated. He had neighbors, but you couldn't see them. Forty acres of sparse trees, mostly junipers, hid them from view. All forty acres were fenced with barbed wire. The top strand razor wire. To get in you had to know the code to the stock gate. When you got out of your car to use the code the first thing you noticed was a pair of cannon, one on each side of the driveway. Most people thought they were relics, not much more than statuary, but Willy knew they fired off just fine.

Once you got through the gate you didn't have to get out again because it automatically closed behind you. A fact both helpful and a little alarming.

The short driveway opened into a wide parking area with a one-story house painted sage green with crisp white trim to the right, and a three bay garage painted to match on the left. A huge US flag hung from a pole between the two buildings. In front of the garage sat a freshly washed, dark blue Dodge Ram pickup and two fishing boats. Willy's dad was big on tidiness, fishing, and America.

"You shoot him?" Was the first thing he asked when Willy got out of his truck and walked up to the house.

Willy hadn't seen him at first. The wide covered porch had a wall around it that just allowed a seated man to see over it. Like most of the elements of The Banker's property, it was that way by design. A survivalist, who anticipated the need to protect him and his from the upcoming apocalypse, Willy's father was prepared.

Did you shoot him? The question made him think of that terrible day, that awful moment.

He remembered how he stared for what seemed like a long time. It was as if his brain refused to register what his eyes were seeing. Then the scene roared into his consciousness. Every detail burning into his memory.

Dodge's body lay sprawled on the floor, arms flung wide, one leg pinning the edge of a tablecloth to the floor. Next to one booted foot lay a handgun, two more were on the table with rifles and gun cleaning supplies.

Willy had wrinkled his nose. The odor of shit and gun oil and the sheared copper smell of too much blood had hit him and his stomach flipped.

The smell reminded him of the slaughter house where his dad yearly delivered the steer he'd raised for meat. Willy had only gone along with his father once. He hadn't been back there since. Once was more than enough.

As he'd stood there trying not to be sick, a rustling sound had reached him. Was there someone else in the house? He'd wanted to turn and run but the thought of someone shooting him in the back as he ran away kept him frozen in place.

There it was again.

The sound broke the spell and he crept, as quietly as he could, toward the back of the house, toward the sound. Just down the short hall off the living room a door stood half open. He nudged it open wider and could see that it was a bedroom. A window was open, the curtains billowing in and out. As they moved they slid across an arrangement of flowers. Long dead, their stems and buds dry, they crackled when the curtains touched them. Realizing that was the sound he'd heard, he sighed with relief. Just to be sure he checked out the rest of the house. Two more bedrooms that looked dusty and unused, a bathroom with damp towels and a moldy smell. He was alone.

As he moved back through the living room and into the dining room he noted that the blood was drying. The spatter, and the edge of the wide pool under Dodge's head, were already turning brown.

He stood over the body for a moment, taking in the wide shoulders and the rodeo belt buckle. Though he'd never wanted anyone dead before, he couldn't say he was sad that Dodge was gone.

Stepping outside, he checked the area. He saw no one. Heard only the creak of the trees moving slightly when the wind gusted, and the sound of crows somewhere in the distance. A new thought struck him and he turned back to the house. Had he left any sign of his presence?

Pushing the sleeve of his jacket down, he wrapped his hand inside the fabric, then used it to wipe his fingerprints from the door and the handle.

Adrenaline was draining from his body. The buzz from the whiskey was fading. He climbed into his truck, started it up, and got out of there. He was happy to leave the house of death in the rearview.

As he drove, he realized he wasn't quite as sober as he'd thought. He had to squint to see clearly. Better be careful. Not a good time or place to get pulled over. Cops tended to frown on drinking and driving. If they picked him up and later found Dodge's body nearby he'd be in trouble.

Hell, if they asked around and found out he'd talked to Bonnie and discovered what she told him. Shit, that would be really bad. They would figure he had every reason to shoot Dodge. What did they call it? Oh yeah, motive. He had motive. Sending him to jail for murder would be the easiest thing they did that year.

"So," his father repeated, breaking into Willy's thoughts, "Did you do it? Kill Dodge."

"What are you talking about?"

"Don't try to play me for a fool. Cops came in and talked to everyone in Muddy Creek they could find. Buddy at the grill called, said they were looking for you. Someone seen you driving around there that morning. You drive your truck up to Dodge's? Damn stupid thing to do in the best of times. Damn stupid. Even for you."

"Thanks, Pop. Kinder words . . ."

"Were never spoken. Yeah, I know. That didn't come out the way I meant it to. You want a beer?" He reached for the green and white Coleman cooler between the two rockers. The old metal cooler had served as both cooler and table on the front porch for as long as Willy could remember. Its top was covered with dark rings from beer cans and coffee cups. Its sides were scratched and had more than a few dents, some from Willy ramming his Tonka Trucks into it.

Nostalgia. It settled over him at the funniest times. All it took this time was the sight of that old cooler. Sometimes it was a song on the radio, or the scent of lilacs. The flowers always made him think of the mother he'd never known. His favorite picture of her, she was standing in front of a row of lilacs, a basket of the cut flowers hanging from her arm. She had her chin down, her eyes looking straight at the camera, the most contented smile on her lips. It was as if the photographer had caught her just after she'd taken a deep breath of her favorite scent, then looked up. He had captured a moment of joy.

He wished he'd had a chance to know her. His father, if he'd ever had the capacity for joy, had lost it somewhere along the way. Just as he was slowly losing his military bearing. Once tall and athletic, he'd begun to let himself go and now, at sixty, he slouched and plodded. He liked to pat the roll of fat around his stomach, bragging that he'd grown it himself. His face looked puffy and he was sweating, even though it wasn't warm and he hadn't done more than reach for a beer. Maybe that was what aging did to everyone. Or maybe it was what happened when people didn't have anyone to make them care.

"Well, did you shoot him?" he asked yet again.

Willy shook his head, "I did drive up there," he admitted, "but no, I didn't shoot him."

"Well that's good, I guess. Assuming you're not lying, but what kind of business would you have with

Dodge?" He left the sentence hanging there. Didn't add anything about Willy using drugs, which was what Willy had expected his father to accuse him of next.

Willy looked him in the eye, "I was up there taking some firewood to Leena, Gordon's wife. She's living in Jansen's Mill."

Willy's father scrubbed his fingers through his short gray hair. "Damn. Sorry to hear that. Not surprised of course. My brother always was as worthless as ice cubes in Alaska. Nope. Not surprised. So, you took it upon yourself to step in I take it?"

"I did," Willy agreed. "Had some firewood, figured they might want to trade for it. Leena's kid, Bonnie, is old enough to work. Thought she could clean the truck or the cabin or something."

"Least you were smart enough to figure out her mother wasn't going to do anything for you. Last I heard she was doing drugs and sleeping around."

"You heard that and didn't check to see how her kid was doing?" Willy asked. "She's your niece." He waited, hoping to hear an answer that would make him less ashamed of his crazy old man.

"Don't go staring at me like that. She isn't my kid

and she sure as shit isn't my responsibility."

"You taught me family is what matters. That we gotta look out for each other," Willy said, daring to correct him.

"Family ain't necessarily blood. My brother, his slut of a wife, and whatever sad creature they spawned isn't mine or yours to worry about. Let's get that clear right now. My family is a handful of my friends that I can trust, and you. You're family and we gotta focus on getting you out of here before this killing blows up in your face. They catch you they'll cage you for the rest of your life."

"I told you, I didn't kill Dodge."

"Don't matter, they know you were up there. They need someone to hang this on. You'll be behind bars before you can say, fuck me."

Willy hesitated. Would telling his father what had happened to Bonnie do any good? His father had ignored his brother's wife and kid. Despite what he said, Willy thought that finding out Bonnie was raped would bring his dad a good dose of guilt and regret.

He had mixed feeling about whether that was a good thing or not. One thing he was sure of, Bonnie wouldn't want what she'd gone through talked about. For her sake he decided to lie. He said, "Leena told me she thought Dodge was looking to buy some firewood, so I drove up there to ask him if that was true."

"Why not just call him?"

"I—I tried. My phone was dead. Keep forgetting to charge the thing."

"They make chargers that plug right in your car now, you know," his father said with the smugness of an older person given an opportunity to teach new technology to a younger one.

"Yes, thanks, I know. I don't happen to own one."

"You got answers for everything, don't you son, only you aren't all that quick off the mark. If your own father don't believe you, what do you suppose the cops will think? Whatever you went to Dodge's house for, that's your business, but you'd better come up with a better answer."

More as a distraction than because he wanted one, Willy reached down and took a beer from the cooler. "You really think the cops are going to come talk to me?" he asked casually.

In response, Willy's father opened the cooler, dug into the ice, and came up with a zip lock freezer bag. Inside was a .38 special Willy immediately recognized.

His father removed the gun from the bag and handed it to him. The steel was as cold as the ice it had been hidden beneath.

"Yep, my holdout gun. I want you to have it. Here, this too." He reached into his back pocket and pulled out a thick leather wallet. Opening it he thumbed out two bills then held them out.

Willy took them as gingerly as he had the gun. Two twenty dollar bills. He looked at his father.

"Get out of town and lay low," his father said.

Willy glanced at the money again and then at the new truck in the driveway. A truck he knew had cost somewhere north of sixty thousand dollars. Paid for in cash. The money said, go away kid, don't bother me. The gun said, this is your problem, go deal with it.

His father cleared his throat. Maybe he was expecting a thank you.

Willy popped the top off his can of beer, took a foam-filled sip. Then he stood up and handed the money back to his father. "I'm good," he said. Then, raising the beer in a salute of sorts he said, "Take care of yourself. No wait, you always do."

He walked quickly to his truck, leaving his father sitting there looking baffled. Nothing new there. He was always surprised that his son, his own flesh and blood, couldn't seem to understand that a man had to take care of himself first.

Willy drove with one hand on the wheel and one wrapped around the can of beer. When he reached the gate the electronic eye saw him, and the gate swung open for him. Before rolling through he tossed the empty can out the window. No doubt his dad would want the nickel.

CHAPTER EIGHTEEN
Thursday, September 13

On Thursday morning, Emma headed to Summer Creek Apartments, four eightplexes that faced each other around a cul-de-sac off Summer Creek Street, the street where Grace Evers lived.

The apartments were all painted the same blend-into-no-background-ever-imagined beige. Luckily they were numbered well and Emma had no trouble finding Building C, Apartment 115.

Grace was an older woman, probably in her early seventies. She was short and slender but not skinny. Her hair was dyed light blond and tightly permed. For a second Emma wondered whether she and Norma Mackie shared the same hairdresser. She wore square, black glasses, a light beige blouse over dark beige pants and a white sweater. She flashed a friendly, slightly gap-toothed smile when she saw Emma. Her movements were animated, fingers darting nervously from the frame of the door, to shake Emma's hand, indicating, with a wide sweep, that she should enter.

Emma did, and found herself in a small but beautifully decorated apartment. Nothing beige here. The walls were sunny yellow lined with white bookcases filled with books, colored glass birds, and framed photographs. A couch and two chairs arranged on a blue rug formed a seating area, like an island floating in the center of the space.

They took seats, Emma on the couch.

"You have a beautiful home, Mrs. Evers," Emma said, and meant it. She took a quick glance at the open kitchen. It was spotless. A glass table and four white wicker chairs sat under a window. On the table a lemon-colored pitcher held an arrangement of blue hydrangeas.

"Thank you," she said, and nervously straightened her sweater. "Please call me Grace."

"Thank you, Grace," she said, and smiled at the small, anxious looking woman. She hoped she could take some of that anxiety away. "I brought my equipment with me," she said, glancing at her purse, which she'd placed on the floor beside her feet.

She removed the camera she planned to use. It looked like a phone charger. I'll connect this and then I'll be able to see what's going on in your apartment twenty-four seven."

"You won't put one in the bathroom!" Grace asked, seemingly aghast.

Emma wasn't sure if she was kidding, but in case she wasn't she reassured her, "No, not the bathroom, or your bedroom. Actually we don't want you to be triggering it all day either so I think, if we just have it watch your front door that would be best. You did say you think he's coming through the door, right?"

"Yes, that's right. He has a key."

"Then we don't need to cover the whole apartment. We'll cover the door and if he comes in we'll catch him."

That's wonderful. Can I offer you some coffee, or tea?"

Emma had noticed the apartment smelled like coffee, with a side of lemon furniture polish, when she entered. She knew that letting someone do something for you was often the best way to put them at ease.

"Coffee would be fantastic."

"Cream and sugar?"

"Just cream. Thank you. This won't take long. Is there an outlet near the door I can use?"

Grace pointed one out and Emma got busy digging out a power cord and powering up the small spy camera.

"I think having it on a cord out in the open makes it look more like a charger and less like a camera. Plus, we don't have to worry about a dead battery. If your power goes out, it does have a battery backup," she explained.

"It sounds so clever," said Grace, as she mixed milk into the cup of coffee she'd poured for Emma.

"It is clever. I'm sure it will help us catch this terrible maintenance man, or whoever has been getting in. Don't worry. We'll put a stop to it fast."

"I believe you," said Grace.

Emma placed the camera on one of the bookcase shelves then took out her phone. Once she connected to the device she looked at the image on her phone and moved the camera around until she had the angle she wanted, a full shot of the door.

"There, now you can walk around in your apartment freely. The only time the camera will see you, or anyone else, is when they're in this space." She indicated the area between the edge of the blue rug and the front door. "Does that work for you?"

"Yes, that's perfect," said Grace. "If you'd join me in the dining room we can have our coffee."

Emma saw that Grace had placed their cups and a plate of some sort of cookies on the table. She knew she should get to the office but company, and cookies, were worth a short delay.

CHAPTER NINETEEN

Thursday, September 13

After leaving Grace Ever's apartment, Emma drove to her office and got busy typing up a report that should have gone out days earlier. She decided to go easy on herself. Finding a body and getting caught up in the investigation of a murder seemed like a pretty valid excuse for being late. She was sure her client would understand.

Plus, she gave herself points for doing anything other than look for Willy Keene's home or talk to Harry Olstad. That would be much less boring than writing a report but, she reminded herself sternly, paying the rent had to come first.

The phone rang, and Emma was surprised to find Leo on the other end. For a hold-your-breath moment she thought he was calling to ask her out. When he said he had some information on the case she was working she wasn't sure whether she felt relieved or disappointed. She decided to give it more thought later and said, "You mean information on the arson?"

"Sure, the arson. Is that what we're calling a shotgun blast to the face these days?"

She didn't answer, just held the phone and listened to the silence.

He broke it first. "Do you want to meet somewhere, maybe get some coffee?"

"Sure, how about Sammy's?" she said, naming a small locally-owned coffee shop she thought was about half way between her office and VR Tactical.

"Perfect. Half an hour?"

She'd agreed and now sat staring at him over her cup. She noted that his dark eyes were the same shade as a dark roast, his skin the same shade as a caramel latte. Lifting the mug, to hide her amusement at all the coffee metaphors, she peered over the edge. Today Leo wore a teal t-shirt with Florida Marlins written across the front. He also wore an unzipped hoodie he kept on even though it was warm in Sammy's. Probably to hide his gun, she decided. Had she remembered to put hers in her purse this morning? No, she was pretty sure it was still locked in the safe at her office. No wonder her sister was always worried about her safety.

Putting down her cup, Emma said, "You have some information for me?"

"Well here's the thing. I got to thinking that your sister and I hadn't done any advertising in Muddy Creek, and I should probably take some flyers and some discount cards out there. So yesterday I did and since I was there anyway . . . "

Emma's brows rose but she didn't say anything.

"I went to a few places and got them to hang our flyer. Asked a few questions. Nothing. Then I stopped at the local watering hole to hand out some cards."

"Because guns and drinking are such a good combination."

"Exactly," he said dryly. "So I had a few drinks, bought a few rounds and, when they closed the place down a couple of the guys invited me over. We ran out of booze so switched to weed. After a few bowls everyone was best friends and very talky."

"Let me guess what they were talking about."

"I didn't even need to bring it up. Dodge's murder is the main subject of all the town gossip. Everyone has their own theory and suspect."

"Do we have any consensus on a winner?" Emma asked. She'd broken off a part of the marionberry muffin she'd bought but was too intent on what he was saying to eat it.

"Have you ever heard of the Padillo brothers?"

Emma shook her head. "I don't think so. Maybe. It's vaguely familiar but nothing I can put my finger on."

"They're two brothers involved in the local drug trade. The older brother, Ernesto, runs a network of dealers, and the younger one, Miguel, helps out."

"I learned, from my own research, that Dodge was involved in the drug trade," she said.

"Your research was correct. My understanding is that, In this county, aside from the random person selling a little weed or some pharmaceuticals, there are three main networks. Dodge is part of a group of Native Americans. The Padillo brothers are part of a group of Mexican Americans, and there's a third group of white guys. The Native Americans mostly sell a little powdered coke, hash, weed and meth. The Mexicans sell heroin, crack cocaine, and meth. The Caucasians sell weed, hash, mushrooms and meth. They all sell oxy and other pharmaceuticals when they can get it. The three networks seem to get along by having pretty clearly defined product and territories. Oh, and you'll love this. There seems to be a long-standing belief, almost a legend, that the district attorney is the one who supplies most of them."

"You learned all this hanging out with some guys at a bar?" Emma asked.

"No, I learned a lot of this on the range shooting with local law enforcement people and the rest smoking bowls with some guys in Muddy Creek last night. You want to know a trade secret? Too much alcohol tends to make people want to fight. Too much weed makes them want to talk."

"Then hurrah for weed." She popped the piece of muffin in her mouth.

"What I heard that was most interesting, besides the DA nonsense, is that there's wide agreement your guy was killed by one of the Padillo brothers."

"Why do they think that?"

"Your guy was—"

"Please don't call him my guy," Emma said, breaking off and eating another bite of muffin.

Leo smiled, "Okay, Dodge, had a reputation for keeping his people in line by—," he looked around then lowered his voice, "by using rape as a punishment. They told me if you stepped out of line, stole his money or his product, you could expect a visit. Only instead of breaking your leg or shooting you, his thing was rape."

"That's horrendous," Emma whispered, matching her lowered tone to his.

"It is," agreed Leo. "One of the guys I was hanging out with said there was a rumor that three or four months ago Miguel Padillo was caught selling at Pine Valley High. That's the more rural of the two high schools and is supposed to be WIP's territory. Oh, that's what Dodge calls his group, We Indigenous People. Charming isn't it."

"Yes, I'm sure all the indigenous people want their name appropriated by drug dealing thugs."

"Drug dealing rapist thugs," Leo corrected.

Emma could tell he was trying to lighten the mood

but it wasn't working and he knew it.

"The rumor is that when Dodge found out, he went to Miguel's, tied him up and was raping him when his wife came home. Miguel broke loose, and was trying to get to his gun cabinet when Dodge shot him dead."

"Jesus. How did he get away with it? Why isn't he locked up? Didn't the man's wife call the police or anything?"

"I don't know but I'd guess that Dodge, or someone, threatened her. In any case, nothing happened. It was written up as an accident. Man shoots himself while cleaning his gun. The rumor is that Dodge left the gun there for the cops to find."

"A gun that was owned by him? Wasn't it registered in his name?"

"Not many people in these rural communities register guns. They swap them, inherit them, buy them at garage sales. Odds are they could never match that gun to Dodge. I'm guessing he's pretty good at covering his tracks. They say Miguel wasn't the first person he killed. Of course this is gossip and rumor but that doesn't mean there's not some truth to it."

"Let me get this straight. The theory is, Dodge

raped and killed the brother of a man who runs an illegal drug operation and was killed because of it?"

"That's what I heard from my new friends."

"Well, I think the information you've gotten from your, 'new friends.'" she said, making quotation marks in the air, "is a lot more than what I've been able to get from the people I've talked to."

"Who have you been talking to?" Leo asked.

"The same people the police have, more or less." She explained about the four individuals seen driving through Muddy Creek that Sunday morning. "I only managed to talk to two of them, Tonya Mackie and Rose Jamison. Neither one seemed like a suspect to me. One was old and sort of frail, the other was, well too polite. I know, I know," she said, putting up her palm. "Nice people kill people. Anyway, the other rancher wasn't around and the kid, Willy, lives way out, down some back road in the middle of nowhere. When you were in town did you happen to stop at the gas station?"

"No. Why do you ask?"

"A woman who works there told me she thinks anyone planning to kill Keller wouldn't be dumb enough to drive through town. They'd have hid their car and walked or, get this, rode a horse."

"Sounds like a pretty good theory."

"I thought so too. Of course now I have to think about all the possible ways someone could have got to that house. It won't be as easy as looking for someone in a car."

"True, but it's not that different right? It's still a matter of finding out if anyone was seen near Dodge's house around the time he was shot. Maybe one of the people you talked to saw someone or something. Maybe they heard the shot."

"Oh my God, the shot. I never even thought to ask."

Leo must have seen the dismayed look on her face. Reassuringly he said, "You would have thought of it. You're smart. Plus remember, you're the good guy. It's the bad guys who always screw up."

"That's not a thing." Emma said.

"It is too," Leo argued. "Don't you watch television? The bad guys always do something stupid. They leave fingerprints, drop their driver's license, or they brag, because they've got to show off. Someone overhears them and tells someone else and if you're actively pursuing it, they might feel more comfortable talking to you, since you're not a cop."

"And I'm a good guy."

"Exactly," he said, but then his smile fell away. "Just remember, the person who committed the crime will also know you're asking questions. That could put you in danger. Have you thought about that? Your job was to investigate an arson, not a murder. Maybe you should drop it. I mean, no one would blame you. Like I said, it's not your job."

"Drop it. Why should I drop it? Because I didn't think about people hearing the shot. Or did you and my sister have a little chat and decide I couldn't do this? You're just like that detective. You think I'm not a professional. That I can't—"

"Man, your sister was right, that bastard did a number on your self-esteem."

"Excuse me," Emma said. Her hands were clenched into fists, each word clipped. "What exactly has my sister told you?"

The thought of El and Leo sitting around talking about her past was infuriating. Her voice had risen. She noticed more than one person sneaking sidelong glances and sat back in her chair, forcing herself to at least look calm.

Leo picked up his coffee, took a long sip, then said. "Your sister wasn't gossiping behind your back. She was upset, and needed someone to talk to. Apparently the idea of killing your husband wasn't out of the question for her. She knew that wouldn't ultimately help you and she needed someone to talk her down before she got on the plane. The risk of running into him was too high.

"The two of us were driving back from a meeting with our financial advisor when the hospital called and told her what was going on with you. I was there, so she confided in me."

"I see," said Emma, and after a few calming breathe, she actually did. "Sorry. I should try harder to control my temper. I have a hair trigger, especially where Mark's concerned. He pushes my buttons, which makes sense, since he installed most of them." She tried for a smile but it came out a grimace. "Let's talk about something else. For instance, tell me why you and El set up your business here? Hollis isn't exactly a center of industry."

"Why not? Oregon is beautiful. Hollis is a few hours from the beach, or skiing, or boating, or whatever you want. Besides, this is gun country. Lots of hunters and target shooting so plenty of customers."

"So it wasn't just because I live here?" He couldn't know what the answer to that question meant to her. She'd tried to make it sound like something she'd casually tossed out but it was much more than that.

Ever since El had announced she was starting a business Emma had wondered, why Hollis? Was it solely because of her? Did El feel she had to be close by to take care of her? Had it driven her to make a terrible business decision? If it had, and the business failed, it would be her fault. If El was unhappy, it would be her fault. Her fault because, after she found out about Mark, she'd temporarily lost her mind.

Her memory of the two weeks after her breakdown was spotty. She remembered discovering and finally accepting the depth of Mark's betrayal. Then she remembered things as strange fragments. Like leftovers from a bad dream. There was breaking glass. Blood. Screams that she came to understand were her own. There was a ride in an ambulance with flashing lights but no sound. The sharp smell of antiseptic. The sharper sting of a needle.

After she woke, they gave her a supply of bitter white pills to keep her numb until she could bear to feel again. She remembered El arriving to take her home. Mostly, she tried not to think about it. It was painful. There was shame there. A huge sense of failure and weakness.

El had gone away when her leave ran out, returning to her job with the military. When, a few months later, she announced her plan to leave the service, move to Hollis and start a business. Emma had been both overjoyed and horrified. She wanted her sister near, but not if was only because she thought Em might have another breakdown.

"Just because you live here?" Leo was saying. "I'm sure that was part of it. But mostly, we were both sick of moving from base to base. We thought it might be interesting to put down some roots, be part of a community. Ellen had lived in Hollis and liked it. That small town feeling and all the outdoor stuff sounded good to me. We'd both seen enough big cities to last a lifetime. I've heard you talk about Portland like it's some kind of metropolis. I'd love to show you Beijing or Moscow."

Emma felt relieved. She thought what Leo said sounded like the truth. Her breakdown wasn't the only reason for her sister setting up business in Hollis. Maybe not visiting VR Tactical had been a way of avoiding her sister after all. That would have to change.

She felt elated. As if a huge weight had suddenly been lifted. Leo's last words didn't hurt either, 'I'd love to show you Beijing or Mosco.' The prospect of flying to distant cities with the extremely hot man sitting mere inches from her was intriguing.

Then, the sound of her sister's voice filled her head. 'No crushing on my business partner. Mixing business and romance never works.' Of course, as she'd explained to El, he wasn't in her business, at least not yet.

Amused by her own double entendre, she drained the last of the cold and only slightly bitter coffee.

CHAPTER TWENTY
Friday, September 14

Emma called the Chevron Station in Muddy Creek on Friday, learned that Audie was working, and though she could have asked her question over the phone, decided to wait and talk to her in person. She had never liked the phone for interviews. Body language could speak volumes while phones, text, and emails were sadly lacking.

Her plan was to talk to Rose and Ms. Mackie again and hopefully track down Harry Olstad and Willy Keene. She also wanted to see if she could find others in town who might have seen something but she'd start with Audie.

As she drove, Emma thought about the questions she needed to ask Audie. For instance, when she saw the four cars go by, what direction were they going and in what order? Had anyone said they heard the shot?

When she pulled into the station, Audie was at the tanks pumping gas into a white van. Emma pulled into the same parking spot she'd used last time and walked back toward the station. She waved at Audie, who raised the gas nozzle in a funny sort of salute, then went inside the store to wait for her.

After a short time, Audie walked in, took off the puffy jacket she wore, tossed it over a stool behind the counter and put some cash in the register. Then she turned her full attention to Emma.

"Good to see you," she said. "How goes the investigation?"

"Slow," said Emma. "I'm hoping you can help me again. I've got a few more questions."

"Fire away," said Audie. She took a stick of Chapstick from her back pocket and coated her lips.

Once again Emma noticed she was dressed cowgirl style, in a white blouse with mother of pearl buttons tucked into black jeans. She wore a necklace made up of dozens of strands of turquoise and feather earrings dyed to match.

"Have you remembered seeing any other cars in town Sunday morning?" Emma asked. "I mean, other than the ones you already told me about."

"Nope. Just those four."

"Do you remember what order you saw them in, and what direction they were going?"

"I believe I do. I gave it some thought when I talked to the cops the other day. Let me think about it a minute." She shut her eye, frowning in concentration, then opened them and picked up a notepad and pen from the counter.

Emma watched Audie draw a square and then a row of arrows, their tips going in different directions.

"This is the station," she said, tapping the square. "This is the folks driving by. First was Rose heading to work as she usually does. That was early, right after I got here, so maybe five-thirty or six. Then, soon after, I saw Norma heading out. I got busy then but around ten I saw Harry's truck go by. He looked to be heading home. Then, it must have been around noon because I just finished lunch and was going out for a smoke, I saw Willy heading toward the highway and Norma heading home."

"So you saw Norma leave and return. Are you sure you didn't see anyone else twice?"

"I don't think so, but that doesn't mean much. If I'm not outside pumping gas I'm inside restocking beer and wine and filling up bags of ice. Plus I have to dust the shelves. I don't have that much time to look out the window. Sorry I can't help more."

"You've been a ton of help. I just haven't been asking the right questions. I'm going to try and talk to the people you saw that morning. I found Mr. Olstad's place last time and I left a note but he hasn't called me back. I still have no idea how to find Mr. Keene. His phone isn't listed. Probably too young to have a landline. Everyone is moving to cell phones now."

"That's for sure. You know, I'm pretty sure Leena Keene, out at Jansen's Mill, is his aunt. I can't swear to it but they have the same last name, and it's not that common.

"The place they live. It's a little sort of trailer trash dump just south of here. You might go out there and ask around. It's so small someone is bound to know which house she lives in. Like I said though, it's not a real nice neighborhood. You might want to take someone with you. I'd think twice about knocking on doors out there alone. Would you like me to draw you a map? I've had to drop off groceries out there a couple times. The store does deliveries to seniors sometimes."

"That would be really helpful," said Emma gratefully, and watched Audie sketch on the notepad.

After buying a diet Dr. Pepper and a slice of apple pie, Emma drove to Mrs. Mackie's, and was happy to find her at home. This time the elderly woman insisted that she come inside.

"How would you like a cup of coffee and a Danish? I picked some up at the new bakery in Hollis on Sunday. They're a tiny bit stale but they're fine if you dip them in coffee."

Emma sat at the table nibbling her pastry and taking small sips of coffee. Even with a splash of milk and two cubes of sugar it was strong. They sat quietly, sharing the view through the dining room window of the wide river rushing by. The quaking aspens along the bank dropped their dying leaves like silver rain in response to each gust of wind.

"You have a beautiful place, Mrs. Mackie," Emma said. "I'm a little jealous."

"I've been blessed, and please call me Norma," Mrs. Mackie said. "What was it you wanted to ask?"

Emma shifted into working gear. "You said you saw Willy Keene Sunday morning. You were driving from your house toward town and he was headed the opposite way."

"No, that's not right," Norma corrected her. "I was coming home when I saw him."

"Oh. When you said morning I just assumed you meant when you were heading out of town."

"No, you're right, I did say that. But now that I think about it I was wrong. I had been to breakfast and the hair dressers and was heading home. No, it wasn't morning, it had to be closer to noon."

"I see. So he was leaving Muddy Creek. I know your place, the Olstad place and Dodge's ranch are up that way. Is there anything else that you can think of that would give him a reason to be up there?"

"Well, sure. We get lots of folks going up into the canyon country scouting deer or birds. Bone Creek has some good fishing too. It's Deer Bone Creek but the locals just call it Bone Creek, Bone Ridge. You know how it is."

"I do. Is he the only one you saw? I remember you telling me he was all over the road and that was probably made you remember him so clearly. Now that some time has gone by, have you remembered anyone else, someone who didn't stick in your memory?"

"Well, I guess if I did, and it didn't stick, I wouldn't be able to tell you," she said, with a wide smile.

Emma laughed. "Yeah, I guess so. Dumb question. Here's another one for you. Did you hear a gunshot on Sunday morning? I'm told Dodge was killed with a shotgun so it must have been very loud."

Norma pointed to her ear, and looking close, Emma noticed the hard plastic bulb of a hearing aid.

"I don't have them in all the time. Not at night, and not until after my shower," she explained. "I'm sorry, but I didn't hear a thing."

"That's all right. I still have a few people to ask. I'm heading up to the Olstad place next."

"You needn't bother with that. He won't be home."

"Oh?"

"Harry got in an accident Saturday evening. He was pulling onto the highway and didn't see a truck coming right at him. Harry's eyes are probably about as bad as my ears, and that truck was probably gray. Tell me why that's so popular, cars and trucks the same color as the road? How are you supposed to see them?"

"So h-he's passed away?" Emma asked hesitantly.

"Oh gosh no. He's gonna be fine. Him and his truck got all banged up and went to the hospital. I mean, his truck is in the shop and he's in the hospital. More coffee?" She turned toward the pot that sat on the countertop burbling happily away and awaiting its next victim.

"No thank you," Emma said hastily. "So, if he's been in the hospital since Saturday. Then how is it that the woman at the gas station saw him Sunday?" Emma said, partly to herself.

"That's a good question, but it couldn't have been Harry she saw. Rose, she's my neighbor and a nurse at the hospital, said she looked in on him. He's got a busted collarbone and a broken arm. They were keeping him in for a few days. Maybe someone was doing him a favor and took his truck home?"

Again, partly musing to herself, Emma said, "But if it was wrecked on Saturday how could it be fixed by Sunday? When I got into a fender bender and needed a tiny bit of body work it took three weeks. Besides, it was a weekend. Who works on weekends? There has to be a mistake. I bet it was a truck that looked like Mr. Olstad's. It couldn't have been his."

"If you ever saw Harry's truck you'd never mistake it for someone else's. That truck is one of a kind. Big white Chevy, big winch on the front, the bed is cherry red, driver's door is blue. I've never seen another one like it. Everyone out here knows Harry's truck. It's like a unicorn in a herd of donkeys."

Emma unconsciously rubbed at the lines that had formed in her forehead. She'd have to talk to Audie again. Getting up, she took her cup to the kitchen, rinsed it and put it in the sink. "I should get going."

Norma said, "If you wanted to know more about Harry you might stop and talk to Rose. She might be able to tell you if he's still at the hospital."

"Do you mean Rose Jamison?"

"Why yes? She's such a nice woman, and her and her husband are such good workers. As a matter of fact, her husband works for Harry now and then. Why, he just might be taking care of the place while Harry's laid up. If anyone brought Harry's truck home I bet it was Charles. Would you like directions?"

"No thank you, that's not necessary. I spoke to Rose the last time I was out here. I was under the impression that her husband would be out of town for a long time. I don't think he could have been driving Harry's truck."

"Hmm, I don't believe he's left town. I saw him just yesterday. He had to come out so he could take some measurements. He's coming over tomorrow to fix a fence that got knocked down by the last windstorm. I've got cows coming at the end of the week and if it's not done they'll end up on the streets. Street walkers." She laughed at her own joke.

Emma laughed politely but her head was spinning with more questions.

"When you went to the house," Norma asked, "did you see all they've done? New paint, flowers planted everywhere. It's going to be beautiful come spring. Like I said, those are some hard working folks. Don't see that in this new generation. They want everything free and easy. You seem like a hard worker though. Trying to find out who killed a man, that not too many are sad to see gone, must be hard. Your list of suspects must be darn long I'd imagine."

"And getting longer by the minute."

Emma thanked Norma and left to find a quiet place to ponder what she'd learned.

CHAPTER TWENTY-ONE
Friday, September 14

Sitting parked in Norma's driveway seemed awkward, so Emma drove out of sight before pulling over and digging a notepad and pen from her purse. Using the steering wheel as a desk, she wrote a rough timeline and some notes.

5:30ish a.m. – Rose seen driving to work.
6:00 a.m. or soon after – Norma driving to Hollis
10:00 a.m. – Harry seen driving toward home.
12:00 p.m. – Willy passes Norma on her way home.

The list led Emma to ask more questions. What was Willy doing up there? When did Rose return? Where was Harry coming from?

Slipping the notepad back in her purse, she put the car in gear and drove toward Rose's. As she drew close she could see there were no cars in the driveway. Too bad but since she was this far out anyway she decided she might as well drive to the Olstad place. She'd love to see if Harry's unique truck had made it home.

Pulling down the dirt and gravel road, Emma immediately noticed gray tendrils of smoke coming from a brick chimney. Someone must be home. It was disappointing to see that the station wagon and RV were still in their respective places but there was no sign of the truck. Maybe there was no one home after all. Still, it was worth trying.

She knocked and was happy to hear a deep voice bellow out.

"Hold on, I'm coming."

The door opened and a man stood in the doorway, looking at her with a half-smile and raised eyebrows. His wrinkled face told Emma he was in his seventies or even eighties but there was nothing else that said he was surrendering to age. His hair was white, but thick, he stood tall, with a sort of relaxed but confident poise as he waited for her to talk.

"I'm Emma Richland," she told him. "I left my business card and a note in your door a few days ago?"

"I didn't see it. Sorry," he told her. "You'll have to tell me what it is you needed."

Emma explained who she was and said, "I've been investigating an arson and it brought me into the investigation of our policy holder's murder. I was wondering if I could ask you a few questions?"

"Well, you could," he said. "Though I doubt I'll be much help. But come on in. Let's at least be warm." He stepped back from the door and Emma noticed he held his right arm tight against his stomach. The left cuff of the flannel shirt he wore was undone and flapped around his wrist. The one on his right was rolled up showing the edge of a cast that stretched his shirt and seemed to encase his arm elbow to shoulder.

She shut the door behind her and followed him down a short hallway that opened to a combination living room and office. In one corner a river rock wall and hearth held a large woodstove. Through a small window she could see flames dancing across a trio of logs, pouring heat into the room. A couple of recliners faced the woodstove and the small television perched on a TV table nearby. The biggest roll top desk she'd ever seen sat against a back wall that was covered from floor to ceiling with ribbons. She couldn't help but stare.

"Horses," he said. "Quarter horses. Cutting horses, barrel horses. My wife and I trained and showed them."

"And you won a lot," Emma said, not failing to notice that most of the ribbons were blue.

"I did."

"You must have loved it."

"We did. Mostly because the sheep and cattle wars are still not over and being a sheep raiser who had the best horses . . . Well, I guess you can figure it out."

Emma smiled. This old man, with his direct gaze and obvious sense of humor, was someone she could fall heavily in like with. "I'd like to ask you some questions about your truck," she said, as she took one of the recliners he indicated.

"My truck?" he asked, a frown forming between his eyes. "Why she's in the shop. I got in an accident out on the highway Saturday. T-boned. My front fender got shoved clean into my tire. Tore it to hell. Put a good dent in the door and along where the gas fill is too. Big mess. So why do you need to know about my truck."

"Well, it's the strangest thing, but the morning Mr. Keller was killed, Sunday morning, your truck was seen going through town heading this way."

Harry shook his head. "No, can't be. She's been in the shop since she got towed Saturday. Tow truck got here about the same time as the ambulance. I remember that clear as day."

"Is it possible someone has a truck like yours"

"Like Maggie? I don't believe so. She's pretty special. You know that old song by Johnny Cash, the one that goes, 'I got it one piece at a time, and it didn't cost me a dime.' Well, that song is about a man who works at a car factory and decides to steal one piece at a time and build himself a car. Only he does it over a lot of years so the parts don't exactly match up right. That's kind of Maggie's story."

"I guess that explains why the bed and cab are different colors." suggested Emma.

"Exactly. I'm pretty sure the driver door is cursed. This'll be her third. Her tailgate and bumper aren't original either, but only car nuts notice that." He gave

Emma another of his smiles. "So who said they saw my truck on Sunday?"

Emma hesitated, then realized in a town the size of Muddy Creek he'd have no trouble finding out.

"It was Audie, down at the Chevron Station," she admitted. The admission had her a little worried. She didn't want him mad at Audie. She also wondered if it was a trick question. His way of seeing whether she'd protect a source or be a rat. She was relieved when his response told her there was no double meaning to his question.

"Oh sure, she'd be in a good position to see most folks going through town. Gal puts in the hours too. Seems like no matter what time I go down there she's the one working. Don't know what her story is though. Hasn't been there long."

He sat musing about Audie until Emma said, "She does seem nice, and she's very attractive."

Harry sat back and slapped his thigh with his good hand, then winced. "Good try, but even if I was twenty years younger she wouldn't be for me. Men always got a type, and she's the only type I ever had." He swept his hand toward the mantel above the fireplace.

Emma noticed a row of photographs that changed, left to right, from black and white to color. In each one the same attractive dark-haired woman with huge brown eyes and generous lips stared at the camera. In each, her expression was both playful and sensual, as if she'd just teased the watcher and was about to run away laughing, but at the same time expected to be followed.

Emma looked at Harry and he looked quickly down and adjusted the cuff on his bad arm.

"Shouldn't you be wearing a sling?" she asked, diverting both of them from the moment of raw emotion that had crossed Harry's face. Emma knew too well how painful it could be to share such things.

"They gave me a sling, yes. but I broke my collarbone as well as dislocating my elbow and it hurts to wear the dang thing."

"Oh, I thought you broke your arm. I guess a dislocated elbow must hurt just as bad."

"Yeah, but they have good drugs in the hospital and it's getting better. Long as I don't bang into anything it's okay. Just funny that the fix for the elbow makes the collarbone worse."

There's a saying in my family, 'The universe has a sense of humor, but it's always ironic."

"There's a saying by Woody Allen, 'If you want to make God laugh, tell him your plans.' "said Harry with a chuckle. "I guess he agreed with your family."

"I guess so."

"Now, back to Audie seeing my truck. It's a real puzzler."

"Could someone have brought it out here? Maybe someone from the shop who wanted to talk to you about the damage or—?" Emma shrugged. She knew her suggestion was unlikely but she had no other ideas.

"On Sunday? Don't seem likely. Like I said, it was pretty smashed up. Quick way to figure it out though." He leaned forward, reached into a back pocket and brought out his cell phone.

Emma internally chastised herself for her ageism. Harry having a cell phone, instead of a landline, had surprised her. Obviously she thought older people were stuck in a time loop. Shame on her.

"The name of the shop is, My Bodyshop. Hard to forget. They're in my most recent list. Here they are."

He punched a button and Emma could hear the muffled ringing as the phone called out.

"Hello, this is Harry Olstad, I'm calling to check on my truck. Yes, that's the one. Right. Yes, that's right, Ingot Silver. No. No. That's fine. Just wanted to check. Say, did one of your guys bring the truck out last week? Muddy Creek. No, I didn't ask . . . Yes, I understand. Of course. No, that's fine. I'll wait for your call. Thanks." He hung up.

"That sounded like a no."

"I think they think I'm a doddering old fart whose mind is going."

He said this with a wide grin, so Emma knew he didn't care what they thought.

"The man who answered said that they will occasionally test drive cars in the area of the shop but never as far out as Muddy Creek. Also, the body work was finished today and Maggie is sitting outside the paint bay awaiting her turn. The insurance is popping for a paint job for the whole truck, so why not," he explained.

"The mystery continues," said Emma. "Well, I'm sorry I bothered you. Guess I'd better get going."

"I'm sorry. I'm a bad host. I'll blame it on the pain pills. I should have offered you a cup of coffee or something."

Emma enjoyed his company but the heat, so welcome when she'd first entered his tidy home, had become hard to bear so she said, "Oh no, that's fine. I've had plenty today. I spent some time chatting with your neighbor, Mrs. Mackie, and she had a pot going."

"Norma gave you coffee, and you're not shaking like a leaf? Must have a good constitution."

Emma nodded, remembering the strong coffee Emma served. "I never believed that expression, "so strong you could stand a spoon up in it," until I had hers."

"I think that saying was written specifically for Norma's coffee." Harry joked. "I'm sorry you had to come all the way out here again. I've been thinking about it, and I'll bet Jelly found your card and note and put them somewhere. He's been taking care of the place while I couldn't."

"Jelly? Is he the one some people call Charles? Married to Rose"

"Sure is. That's his actual name, Charles, I mean

but when I met him he said people call him Jelly, so I have. Jelly," he scoffed. "Awful nickname. Meant to ask him about how he came to get it, but he's not much of a talker."

"So he's been here," Emma said, excited to gain another bit of information. "He's been taking care of your place since when, Saturday, Sunday?"

"Oh, I didn't call anybody Saturday. They knocked me out like a light. Sunday is when I called. Early Sunday morning. Jelly said he had to run his wife to work but he'd come out and take care of things when he got back. He's an early riser, they both are. I've had to deal with night owls all my life and let me tell you, it's a relief to be able to call someone in the morning and know you're not waking them up."

Emma gave what she hoped was a sympathetic smile, then said. "I guess I should get going. You should probably get some rest."

Harry shrugged, then winced again.

"And maybe some of those pills. It was nice meeting you. I hope you feel better soon."

"Don't you worry. They haven't got me just yet."

They stood and Emma said, "Do you mind?" She

gestured toward Harry's loose sleeve. He smiled and held his arm out. Emma carefully rolled up the sleeve he hadn't been able to.

"You'd make a fine nurse," he told her.

"I'd rather be a fine investigator," she told him.

"Bedpans?" he asked, humor shining in his eyes.

"Bedpans," she agreed.

After waving goodbye and driving away from the Olstad place, Emma decided it was time to do as she'd planned. Go back to Muddy Creek and start talking to anyone she could find. There were several questions she wanted to have answered and some things she needed to verify.

First though, she'd make a quick stop at what she was starting to think of as Audie's store. She was in desperate need of a bottle of water and some mints to kill the bitter aftertaste of Norma's poisonous coffee.

Leaving her car at the gas station, she headed on foot down Main Street. Though she stopped at every store, cafe, and business her only win was when she talked to the manager of the community center. He was the elderly man with braids who she'd noticed before. All he could offer was that he'd seen Harry

Olstad's truck Sunday morning. Confirmation was good but something new would have been better.

Once she got back to her car she sat back and thought about what her next steps should be.

Online at her office, she'd found Willy's address easily. When she'd looked at the place using satellite imagery it became obvious how isolated it was. Tracking down a possible killer in the middle of nowhere didn't seem smart. Instead, she pulled out the map to Jansen's Mill Audie had drawn for her. It wasn't very far away.

Spotting the turn off, Emma drove off the highway onto the shoulder of the road a little too quickly and felt her tires slide. She touched the brakes and the car slowed and straightened.

The dirt road to Jansen's Mill was rutted and uncared for making her glad she drove a Jeep. Although it wasn't so rough she had to use the four wheel drive, the extra clearance was useful. Pulling into the driveway of the first house, she got out and looked around cautiously. The neighborhood looked as sketchy as Audie had described. Maybe she should have brought someone with her, at the very least someone to be a lookout for dogs. It was definitely Pitbull territory.

Crossing to the door of the old single-wide trailer which seemed to be rusting slowly away, she knocked. An elderly man came to the door and stared out at her with bloodshot eyes before barking, "What?"

"I'm trying to find Leena, but I don't know which house is hers. I was hoping you could help me."

He rolled his chew from one side of his jaw to the other, turned his head and spit. Emma gave him her brightest smile.

He jabbed his thumb to the left and said, "Two houses down." Then he shut the door and Emma heard the trailer creak as he walked away.

Getting back in her car she drove to the house he'd indicated. It too was a tired single-wide mobile home, leaning slightly, its peeling paint revealing the raw metal beneath.

Climbing the rickety makeshift cinder-brick porch, she knocked on the door. A woman opened it. She was thin, and wore a t-shirt over pajama bottoms and dirty panda slippers. She said nothing, just stood in the doorway, arms crossed, staring at Emma.

"Hi," Emma said, feeling awkward. "Are you Leena Keene?"

"Who are you?" was the woman's reply.

"My name's Emma Richland, I'm a private investigator from Hollis." She reached in her purse, pulled out a business card and handed it to the woman, who took it gingerly, as if it might be too hot to touch. Then she read it, her lips moving.

Looking up, she said, "What do you want?"

"I'm looking for Willy Keene. I'd like to ask him some questions."

"About what?" She pushed up the sleeve of her sweater and scratched her forearm.

Emma noticed the small red scabs on her arms, the deep set eyes. She looked sick, like someone going through a final round of chemo, but the pick marks and a missing canine said it was a different kind of drug that was slowly killing her.

There was a noise inside the trailer. The woman turned her head then turned back to Emma. "He's not here."

"I didn't think he was here. I just need to reach him and thought you might have his phone number."

"Hey Bonnie, do we got Willy's phone number?" She called into the trailer. Then, without waiting for a response, she turned back to Emma and said, "I don't think we got it."

"That's too bad. I'd give you . . ." Emma reached in her pocket and dug out all the cash she had, twenty three dollars and a bit of change. "I'd give you twenty-three dollars if you could find it."

The woman took a step back, said, "One minute," and went into the house, shutting the door behind her. A moment later she returned with a piece of lined paper torn from a notebook. On it had been penciled a phone number. "Here it is," she said, holding the paper against her chest.

Emma got the message and held out the money. The woman took it and handed Emma the triangle of paper. "That's the number he gave my daughter. Should be good."

"Thank you," Emma said, relieved that their interaction was at an end. The woman gave her the creeps and she didn't want to think about the conditions any daughter of hers was living in. She wondered how old the girl was. Maybe she should call someone when she got to town. She'd found family for foster kids and still had a couple acquaintances in social services who might be able to help.

Heading slowly back down the bumpy road, Emma thought about what she'd learned. Though she had a better idea of the time her suspects had been seen, and the direction they were traveling, that information told her very little. Instead there were additional mysteries.

Rose Jamison had lied about her husband being out of town. Why would she do that? What was she hiding? How could Harry Olstad's truck have been seen on Sunday if it was in the shop? Did someone have a truck similar to his? Was that person the killer?

CHAPTER TWENTY-TWO

Friday, September 14

After leaving his father's place, Willy went home and slept in his own bed. He slept hard but woke suddenly, a dream of falling startling him from his sleep. He sat up, rubbed his hands across his face, noticed he needed to shave.

When he'd pulled up to his cabin yesterday afternoon the scattered sheds and shops that held his trade goods had never looked more pathetic. Wind had torn the side off of his greenhouse and the cold had taken care of his sad little marijuana patch.

Inside the cabin, he took off the top of the cookie jar and dug out the cash he kept there. He counted it twice. One hundred and eighteen dollars. With the money in his pocket he was just short of one fifty. That wouldn't get him very far. Certainly not far enough to start a new life.

His father's words came back to him. "They catch you they'll cage you for the rest of your life." He went outside and looked around, for what he thought might be the last time. The wind brought him the smell of pine and something that hinted of snow. His cabin stood at the end of a barely used road, its edges fading into wildness. A squirrel scampered up a nearby tree. Beyond it he could see mountains, one after another rising up all shades of blue gray until they faded into mist. The sky was so blue it made his eyes tear up. Clouds as thin as torn tissue raced endlessly above.

Being locked in a cage, especially for something he never did. That wasn't fair. It wasn't right. He suddenly remembered the bottle of gin someone had traded him long ago. He didn't like gin, but he went in and found it under the sink, took a swig. It made him cough but it wasn't that bad.

He grabbed an old duffle bag and started shoving clothes into it. Tossed it in the cab. He wandered around, packing tools, things he thought he might be able to pawn easily. Then he tied a tarp across the whole mess. By the time he finished ratcheting down the last strap the gin was half gone and he was staggering just a bit. He screwed the top down, slipped the bottle onto the front seat, hidden under his bag but within reach.

The whole time he'd been getting ready to run his mind had frantically leaped from one impossible solution to another.

He needed money. That was the main thing. He considered robbing The Banker. There was a sweet satisfaction in that idea. He thought through the whole thing. How he'd drive up, bust into the truck, cut the lock on the safe, take the bundle of cash. There were probably thousands in there.

Then he remembered the razor wire, the hidden traps. Mostly he remembered his father's stern expression and the one time he'd seen him deal with a thief. Willy couldn't forget the man fumbling to get in his car, his shirt wrapped around his hand, blood dripping on his jeans as he managed to start the car and get the hell out of there.

Two of the man's fingers had been sitting on top of the chopping block near the wood pile for days, until

Willy had gingerly scooped them up with a shovel and buried them.

For a moment, he let himself drift into a fantasy where he held a gun on his father and commanded him to get the money. He'd take it, then order his dad to get on the porch before slowly backing to his truck and driving away.

The only problem was that every time he played that scenario it reset to another one, with him holding the gun while his father laughed his ass off. No way would he be able to bluff that crazy bastard.

The next best plan that came to him wasn't his at all. It was his ex-girlfriend, Krista's idea. When he started dating her, she'd been working at Shirley's Market, a neighborhood store in a Hollis suburb. He'd pick her up and sometimes he'd get there too early so they'd hang out. They'd eat chips and sneak beer out of the cooler, filling up a slushie cup in case a customer came in or they got caught on camera. Luckily the only camera was pointed at the till, keeping an eye on the clerk's sneaky fingers, so that wasn't too hard to avoid.

Once she could leave and they were in Willy's truck, Krista would talk about how easy it would be to rob Shirley's. "Just hide your face, buy an old jacket at the Goodwill, come in and hold a gun on me. I'll be so scared I'll give up all the money in the till. Plus the extra money."

"Extra money?"

She explained that when the till got over two hundred in it, they were supposed to count out the extra, put it in an envelope, and drop it in the safe. Only no one did that. Instead, they'd tuck the envelope next to the till, hiding it in a bunch of paperwork. That way if they ran short they could pull money out of it rather than call the owner, the only one with a key to get into the safe.

Krista said afterward they'd meet and split the money. Willy had always laughed off the idea, pretending she was joking, even when he knew she wasn't.

Then one day he'd shown up at the store and another guy had been there, hanging out with her. He was an older man with a better car. Krista had told him how sorry she was. How she'd found someone else. He was pretty sure she was hoping he'd fight the other guy, or at least act hurt. Instead, he'd looked at her bleached blond hair with its dark roots, a sort of reverse skunk effect. Noticed the black gunk around her eyes and how her lipstick clumped in the corners of her mouth. Then he looked at the guy with her, said, "Good luck," and walked away. It had been the smartest move he'd ever made.

Krista's plan could still work though. He knew about the envelope. Knew the store's cameras. At least as long as they hadn't changed them. He hadn't seen Krista in about a year but he doubted she worked at Shirley's anymore. She wasn't the kind of employee to keep a job for long.

He drove away from his home without looking back. Behind him a cloud of dust rose and hovered in the air. He ran through the plan over and over. What he would say. What he thought the clerk would do. How he would react to. He stopped, looked both ways, then drove from the dirt road onto the highway. He was so deep in thought that he didn't notice the car that drove onto the highway and fell in line not far behind him.

* * *

Inside the unmarked police car the deputy spoke into his cell phone. "I'm heading south on 97, vehicle in front of me, two for cover." This told his team that he was following Willy Keene south, down Highway 97, with two cars between them.

*   *   *

When Willy pulled into the parking lot of Shirley's Market his hands were shaking. He wiped his damp palms on his jeans. *This is dumb. This is a dumb idea.* He put his hand in the pocket of his jacket. His fingers brushed the cold steel of the gun.

There were only two cars in the parking lot. The one parked farthest from the door probably belonged to the clerk. He waited until the driver of the second car, a woman carrying a soda and unwrapping a pack of cigarettes, left the store.

She looked barely old enough to smoke. Her short dark hair had pink streaks. Under a brown corduroy jacket she wore a pink t-shirt. She also had on faded jeans with frayed hems and neon-orange sneakers. Willy realized his brain was working overtime. He was staring at the woman, seeing and cataloging everything about her as if his life depended on it.

Breaking his gaze he sat motionless, staring straight ahead, until he heard her car start up and drive away.

"Time to go," he said under his breath, and climbed out of his truck. His knees wobbled a bit but he forced himself to move.

Once inside, he waited for his eyes to adjust to the dim light. The clerk was male, early twenties, a little heavy. He nodded a welcome to Willy from behind the register, then went back to looking at his phone.

Willy wandered around the store, making sure they were alone. He picked up a small package of chocolate donuts and grabbed a strawberry milk from the cooler. All an excuse to let him circle the perimeter of the small space. No one else was there.

Carrying the items to the counter he set them down. Then, before he could lose his nerve he said "Put the money from the register in a paper bag. I have a gun." The sound of his own voice, so calm and direct, surprised him.

The clerk's eyes went wide and he seemed frozen. Willy spotted a stack of small paper bags on the edge of the counter. He took one and handed it to the clerk.

"Put the money in this. Open the register. Now!"

The clerk jumped, then took a half step to the left and hit a button on the register. The drawer slid open noisily making Willy jump. The clerk reached into the register, pulling out the money, fumbling and dropping some of it as he tried to open the bag and stuff money into it at the same time.

Willy, afraid that someone might drive up, tried to keep his eyes on the clerk and on the parking lot at the same time.

The clerk, his name tag said Brice, tried to hand the bag to Willy but he didn't take it. "The envelope," he said. "The money you keep out so you can refill the till. Get the envelope."

"We . . . we aren't allowed to refill the till."

Willy stared at him, saw his eyes dart to and then away from where Krista said they kept the envelope.

He drew the gun out of his pocket. Brice stared at it, licked his lips. Willy thought he looked scared enough to wet himself but he could understand. The gun's grip was so slick with his sweat he was afraid he might drop it.

"I-I forgot," Brice lied, and reached between the

register and a display of lighters where inventory lists, purchase orders and miscellaneous papers were kept. He pulled out a small manilla envelope.

"Put it in the bag," Willy told him.

Brice did.

"Now hand it to me." Willy took the bag and backed toward the door. "You stay. You stay where you are. You hear me?"

Brice nodded. His face was pale as paper, except for bright pink spots high on his cheeks.

Willy pushed through the glass door, headed toward his truck at a quick pace, the gun held tight against the side of his leg.

The street was quiet. Weirdly quiet. No traffic. No kids on bikes. Nothing. No, not nothing, a squirrel was chirping and in the distance he could hear the sound of a lawn mower.

Willy looked around, scanning the neighborhood, the street. The grange hall, a large community building with a dirt parking lot was across the street.

The sun broke from the clouds. A flash of light caught his eye. Behind the grange he spotted a dark fender, the sun reflecting from the surface of a spotlight mounted on it.

Police. A police car had been backed in, behind the grange. They were there. Hiding. He broke into a cold sweat.

"Fuck."

Everything was still amplified, colors sharper, smells stronger, sounds louder. Only time seemed muffled, strangely slowing.

There was a sound. Something he'd heard before. The soft rattling of a small stone rolling across asphalt, then the scuff of a shoe. He started to turn, saw another police car parked in the driveway of the house next door.

"Hands up! Police! Get your hand's . . . "

Willy heard loud excited voices shouting at him. Orders coming from every direction. Confused and scared, he spun toward the loudest voice. The gun in his hand swung loosely at the end of his arm as he turned.

"Gun!"

The first bullet slammed into his side just above his right hip, traveled diagonally upward and lodged itself just below his left rib cage. It didn't hurt. Willy thought it felt like someone had thrown a snowball at him. Still, something made him go to his knees.

The second bullet tore through his left bicep, smashed into his ribs and knocked him sideways. The gun fell from his hand and skittered across the parking lot.

The third bullet hit his jaw and kept traveling, bone and bullet fragments tearing through his brain and ending his life.

The fourth and fifth bullets punched through his thigh, and although the target was dead, the impact moved the body and one of the officers fired again.

CHAPTER TWENTY-THREE

Monday, September 17

Once more the Major Crime Unit met in the main conference room of the DA's office to discuss the Keller murder. This time there was a different feel to the room. A sort of unspoken sense of a job well done. No one congratulated anyone however. Someone had died. Besides, an officer involved shooting was always a pain in the ass. An internal investigation would take place. Accusations of police brutality would hit the news. However, in this case, no one seemed to think there would be too much kick back. William Keene, Jr. had been armed and was caught in the commission of a felony when he was shot.

"We all know this was a bad guy," Beale said. "Sheriff Plummer, would you mind filling us in?" Beale didn't mind giving the man the room. It was a good move politically and kept the focus off of him, just where he liked it. Besides, he'd met with Plummer to help formulate the narrative so he didn't expect any surprises. There weren't any.

"Our working theory is that this all started in July when that warehouse on Market went up," the Sheriff explained. "You guys remember that?" A few heads nodded. "We now believe that William Keene set the warehouse on fire. The warehouse was owned by Dodge Keller." He paused for dramatic effect, then went on. "The fire was meant to draw Dodge out. We think Keene hid himself somewhere, where he could watch the property. When Dodge arrived he planned to kill him. However, Dodge didn't show up. We think he then came up with a different plan."

"Why do you think Keene wanted to kill Dodge?" someone asked. Beale looked up from the notepad where he'd been doodling but didn't catch who'd spoken.

"For money. We believe he was hired to do so." explained the sheriff. "Ernesto Padillo had threatened to kill Dodge Keller. As most of you know, the Padillos run a drug operation that we, along with the feds, have been investigating for the past year. Keller runs a smaller operation out of the reservation. We got wind of a disagreement between them. When Miguel Padillo committed suicide his brother, Ernesto, blamed it on Dodge Keller."

"Why would he think that Dodge had anything to do with his brother's death?" asked one of the young officers "I remember that. Wasn't it suicide?"

"That's what the coroner said, and that's what we have to go on. What's important to know is that whether it was a suicide or not, Ernesto believed Dodge had something to do with his brother's death and he wanted him dead.

"However, it wouldn't be that easy for him. Dodge had a lot of men paid to protect him. Padillo couldn't drive out to the reservation without being recognized. He knew the smart thing would be to hire someone who could get around out there without being noticed. We think that's why he hired Keene.

"Keene's father is known out there as The Banker. He's the local lender for folks who can't get money the normal way."

"Like a loan shark?" someone asked.

"Exactly," said Sheriff Plummer. "He drives all over that area, and so does his son. No one would have thought twice seeing him out there. Plus, we know for a fact he was there. He was seen by several locals the morning Keller was killed. Doesn't leave much doubt.

"As part of our investigation, we put our special operations team on surveillance in hopes of catching Keene and Padilla in a meeting. A meeting between them would strengthen our case. Instead, Keene was caught robbing Shirley's Market. He brandished a handgun and was shot."

"But why rob a small store if he had just fulfilled a contract to kill someone?" asked one of the deputies. "Wouldn't he have been paid pretty well?"

"That may be another thing we will never understand," offered Beale. "Criminals are not wired the way the rest of us are." He noticed there were nods of agreement all around the table. With this level of unity the meeting should wrap up soon. He hoped so. After all, he had work to do.

CHAPTER TWENTY-FOUR

Monday, September 17

With four people in it, Emma's office was filled to capacity. Emma had rolled her office chair out from behind the desk and they now sat in a circle, El and Gwen in her guest chairs, Leo perched on the edge of the desk. He had one foot tucked under the other leg and was bent toward her, listening. His intense focus left her feeling a little breathless.

She looked at Gwen and continued to fill her in on what had taken place while she was in Hawaii. "The police think it was Willy who set the fire at the warehouse. He was shot when he robbed Shirley's Market."

"It was on the news," Gwen said. "How awful. You have to wonder why someone would make such bad decisions. He was so young and not to sound like a cliché, he had his whole life in front of him."

"I know," agreed Emma. "From the research I did on him, he was a decent student, involved in sports and other activities. It's hard to believe but I guess you never know what's going on in someone's life."

"There's a lot of poverty in this county," suggested Leo with a shrug. "The haves and the have nots. But it's hard to say that's the only reason. A lot of poor kids make it and some rich kids fail. Drugs, alcohol, all kinds of addiction. Seems to be an equal opportunity issue. Money helps, but it's not always enough."

Gwen nodded. "Money isn't everything, that's for sure. Speaking of money, we're going to pay the claim. The police say the fire was set by a third party, this Willy kid, and the policy holder wasn't a party to it, so his estate will get the money."

"At least it's over," said Ellen. "Em won't have to keep looking into it."

"True," said Gwen. "If I'd known the fire was part of a plan to kill someone, I'd never have gotten Emma involved," she said apologetically.

"You couldn't have known," said Ellen.

"Hey, knock it off," said Emma. "I'm sitting right here and you're making it sound like I can't be trusted to take care of myself. This is what I do for a living. You get that, right?"

"Sorry," said Ellen. "Big sister syndrome."

"Me too," said Gwen, "I mean, sorry if I made you feel like that but I still mean it. I would have left this to the cops if I'd known the kind of people you'd be dealing with." Shaking her head she reached into her purse and pulled out a checkbook. She filled out a check and handed it to Emma. "Now take this and don't argue. You did a lot of work and I'm grateful. This is hours, mileage and a tiny bonus, because I'm pretty sure you shorted the invoice on both."

Emma couldn't argue. Gwen was right. She took the check.

The phone rang and as Emma reached for it, Gwen got up, gave a silent wave, and left. Leo slid off the corner of the desk and took the chair she'd vacated.

"Richland Investigations," Emma said.

"He was here. I think he came in last night, while I was at the senior center bingo," said a woman breathlessly.

"Mrs. Evers? Grace?" asked Emma, recognizing the quivering voice.

"Yes. Can you come check the camera now?"

"I'm sorry, Grace. Didn't I explain? I can check the cameras from anywhere. Let me do that now and I'll get back to you, okay?"

"Yes. I'll wait to hear. Just please, hurry."

"Problem?" Ellen asked.

Emma shrugged. "Client of mine. I set up some cameras to try and catch someone she thinks is breaking in, going through her things. I need to check the footage, see if it picked up anything."

"Sounds like you need to get busy. Me too. I've got a group of women coming in for tea-and-target training."

"For what?" Emma asked, incredulously.

"Tea and then targets. What, you've never heard of this before?" she asked with feigned surprise.

At sight of her sister's befuddled expression, Ellen explained. "We sit around, drink tea, eat cookies and watch a PowerPoint presentation about gun safety and then we hit the range. Going to a tea and target shoot, taught by a woman, attended only by women and with no men allowed, makes certain women more comfortable."

"Certain women?"

"Yep. Women who need to learn to shoot but don't have a particular interest in guns. Most of the women in this particular class have never so much as seen or held a gun before and would really rather not."

"But they want to hold one now?" asked Emma,

"Afraid so. Most of them have left an abusive relationship. They're pretty distrustful of men and they know they might be in danger from a former partner. A lot of them heard of us through domestic violence shelters. We also try to put flyers in places women frequent. These particular classes are designed for them."

Emma could relate. Though Mark had never been physically abusive, his lies had hurt deeply and made it nearly impossible to trust. "They must be angry," she said. "Are you ever afraid one will take her training and use it to go after the guy who hit her?"

"No, I just have to hope the training teaches them to be wise enough to avoid confrontation, but to be ready if it happens. The women who attend the teas are all different. Sure, some are angry and aggressive but others are timid as mice. The funny thing is, once we get out on the range, the mousy women are often more badass than the ones that seemed tough. We also get a variety of ages, everything from fourteen to . . . I don't know. How old was our oldest client do you think?" she asked Leo.

"Eighty-three, if I remember right." said Leo.

"Yeah, that was Betty," Ellen said. "Her stepson ripped her off so she hired a lawyer. He found out and slapped her around. Thought he'd intimidated her. He hadn't. She got her lawyer to cut him out of everything and then bought a gun. Sad story."

"But if he shows up in the middle of the night," said Leo.

"She'll be ready," said Ellen. "She mentioned she was thinking of hiring someone to help her find a cousin of hers. Someone she lost touch with but is her only family. She has a pretty nice estate and would like to leave it to the cousin, now that stepson is out of the picture. Interested in helping her?"

"Sure," said Emma, thinking that maybe this was the universe telling her to get back to what she did best. Find people.

"Hand me your phone. I'll put her contact info in it for you. Her name's Betty. Betty Carpenter."

Emma handed over her phone and Leo said, "Enough talk about the store. What about you? You did a lot of work on this investigation. I know how much you wanted to solve the murder."

Emma sighed and leaned back in her chair. "Yeah, I did, but not for a good reason. Not to find justice or anything noble. I just got mad at that detective who gave me attitude. Doing stuff out of anger is not usually a good idea. I need to work on controlling my emotions, especially my temper."

"Don't beat yourself up too much," said Leo. "A lot of people never question their motives for doing things. At least you did and are trying to learn from it."

Emma shrugged. "I guess. I mean, if I'm being honest, I also wanted to investigate the killing because it was interesting. It was something different, and I am a PI after all. We're known for solving murders—at least on TV," she said with a chuckle. "Hey, who doesn't watch Magnum PI reruns?"

Her cell phone, which Ellen was still holding, rang

and Ellen handed it back to her.

"Richland Investigations."

After a moment, Emma set the phone down on the desk without saying anything.

Ellen raised her brows.

"They hung up on me," Emma explained.

"Spammer?"

"No doubt."

"Okay, well I better go," said Ellen. "That tea's not going to brew itself."

Leo looked from Ellen to Emma and said, "I'm not allowed at this particular event, thank God. I'm not even allowed in the building. Want to go to Healy's and shoot pool?"

Emma considered it for a moment. Did he have to be so nice? The packaging was already above average. Being nice too put him right in the dangerous column since she was definitely not looking to get into a relationship.

"Sorry, I can't," she told him. "You heard me promise a client I'd check out something for her. Plus I really need to get to the bank and deposit this check." She waved Gwen's check in the air in front of her and turning her attention to her sister said, "Just think El, rent, groceries, beer!"

"At least you've got your priorities in order," said Ellen.

"Always. Plus, after Mrs. Evers, I should call this Mrs. Carpenter of yours before she finds someone else."

"And before the beer, I hope," said her sister.

"Party pooper."

"Hey, Vargie," Ellen said to Leo, "Would you go start the car?"

A wide grin made Leo's eyes sparkle. "You hear this? Vargie, not Vargus. She clearly wants something. Hola Vargus, mi querido amigo. Mi querido compañero. Mi querido. Mi asso." He puckered his lips and pantomimed kissing with loud smacking sounds, then, with a small but well-executed bow he left, closing the door firmly behind him.

Ellen and Emma smiled at the exaggerated expression of grievance.

"What did you want to tell me that he couldn't hear?" Emma asked.

"It's the key fob," said Ellen, wasting no time. "My

friend at the FBI called tonight. The fob was too damaged to get a unique number that would let him trace it to a particular car, but he had no doubt about the kind of car. It belonged to a Tesla."

"Tesla huh. Can't be many of those around. You have to head toward Portland or down to San Francisco to find the kind of money and people who buy Teslas. It's strange."

"Definitely," said Ellen, as she got up, rolled her shoulders and then headed toward the door. "I guess it doesn't matter now. It's going to be one of those puzzles that doesn't get solved. The one person who knows the answer is dead. Let me know what happens with Mrs. Campbell. She's a good person."

"I Will," Emma promised.

Once Leo and Ellen were gone, Emma rolled her chair back to its usual place behind her desk. Then she opened the hidden camera's app on her phone. The files she wanted were in a folder, each labeled with a date, and time stamped. There were five files and she played each of them twice. They were basically identical.

Each scene began with a blur of movement that quickly resolved into the figure of a woman. The woman was easy to identify as Grace Evers. She went out around nine in the morning and returned around eleven for two days. On the third day, today Emma realized, she left but had not returned. There was no other activity. No one else had entered the home. What a relief.

Emma created a new folder, named it Grace Evers, and moved all the digital files into it. If Grace wanted a copy she could easily text or email them to her.

With a flip of her finger she shut the app and then dialed Grace's number. She answered on the second ring.

"Hi, It's Emma Richland. I have good news. No one has entered your apartment since I installed the cameras."

"But he had to. Things have been moved, and like I told you, I can smell his cigar."

"Maybe what you smell is smoke drifting in from outside or from another apartment," suggested Emma reasonably.

"No, it's not that," Grace insisted. "I'm afraid that

you just proved what I've suspected for a while now."

"What's that?" Emma asked, her curiosity aroused.

"That he can make himself invisible. I sort of wondered about that. If you met him you'd understand. He's sort of sly. Sometimes he'll give me this look, like he knows something I don't. You know what I mean, a sort of sneaky look?"

"He can . . . He what?" asked Emma, realizing she was stuck on the invisible part of the story and unable to move on to concern about his sly or sneaky look.

"It's okay," Grace said. "I know it seems strange but if you think about it, what else could it be?"

Emma didn't know what to do or say and realized she was sitting there with her mouth wide open. For the first time in her life she understood the expression, a jaw-dropping moment.

"H-he . . ."

The realization, that her latest client was paranoid and delusional, had momentarily taken her ability to form a full sentence.

Misreading the cause of Emma's stutter, Grace said, "Don't be afraid. I know it's very strange and creepy but the thing is, I think he's ex-military. I'll bet he was part of some kind of military experiment. These things happen."

Emma managed to get through the rest of the conversation. She told Grace that given what they knew, she felt it would be wrong to take her money. There was really nothing she could do. She'd be tearing up her check and hoped she'd work things out with the maintenance man.

"But we could set another trap," Grace suggested. "I'm thinking maybe if we sprinkled flour on the floor and you put the camera where it could see his footprints we'd have him."

Emma said she'd think about it and hung up.

"Oh boy, am I ever going to get that camera back?" she asked the empty room. She scrubbed her fingers through her hair then took a deep breath, which triggered a yawn.

More coffee. Coffee was always the answer. Before she could get up to start a fresh pot, the phone rang. Dreading that it would be Grace calling back to ask for help in tracking her invisible man, Emma looked at the screen. It showed a local number but not one she recognized.

"Richland Investigations," she said.

"He-hello," a girl's voice hesitantly responded. "Is this Emma Richland?"

"Yes, it is."

"M-my name is Bonnie. You gave my mom your phone number. My mom, L-leena?"

"Leena. Willy Keene's aunt." said Emma, coming alert as she realized who she was talking to.

"Yes, th-that's right."

"What can I do for you, Bonnie?" Emma picked up a pen and scribbled the name on the edge of her desk calendar.

"They shot my c-cousin." Bonnie said. "The cops I mean."

"Yes, I'm sorry. I heard about that," said Emma, as gently as she could. The girl was nervous, even frightened. She expected her to hang up at any moment, but she didn't, and her next words came in a rush.

"They said he killed Dodge Keller but he never did. He couldn't have. I heard the gunshot. I could see Willy in his truck. How could he be in his truck and shoot the gun? He couldn't. He didn't do it."

Emma felt a shiver run down her spine. She held the phone tighter. "Where are you?"

It was dark by the time she reached Leena's trailer. A young girl she guessed was about thirteen or fourteen opened the door and introduced herself as Bonnie. She was slender, a couple inches shorter than Emma, with long brown hair and big brown eyes, one of which sported a hell of a black eye. It was a vivid purple, fading around the edges to an ugly pinkish green.

Emma wasn't completely surprised to find such a young person left alone in this rough place, in the middle of nowhere, after all she'd met her mother.

"Mom went to town, to work. She got a job at the casino. We can talk."

Bonnie had opened the door and stood aside, an invitation for Emma to enter. She'd done so, taking a seat on the recliner while Bonnie perched on the arm of the couch. The recliner listed to one side and Emma could feel her spine protesting. She ignored it. Bonnie's story was too mesmerizing to allow her to concentrate on anything else. She'd been telling the story of her cousin Willy's unexpected visit.

"After we got the wood unloaded he gave me ten dollars. He told me it was a tip for doing such a good job and to buy something for me, not give it to my mom. Like I would. I didn't buy anything either. I put it in my bank."

"Good for you. Saving is a great habit and your cousin sounds like a nice guy. You told me he couldn't have shot Mr. Keller. How do you know that?"

"Because I was looking right at him when I heard a shot. I'm pretty sure it must have been the one that killed Dodge. It was the only shot I heard that day. Everybody knows Dodge likes to target shoot, and since his mom died, it's gotten worse. His friends come over and then it's blam, blam, blam.

"Nobody walks over the ridge when they start shooting over there. You gotta walk down to the highway and go that way. You can always tell when they're shooting though. It's loud and sometimes you can even hear voices, yelling and laughing and stuff.

"All I heard was the one shot and that was kind of weird. I guess I thought it was a hunter maybe, until I found out Dodge got killed. Then they said Willy shot him, but if he did, I sure didn't hear it, and I was here all day. I know you probably don't believe me."

Emma could see the frustration on her face. "I believe you heard a shot, if that helps. Tell me exactly where your cousin was and what he was doing when you heard it?"

"He was in his truck, just a little way down the road. I could still see him clear as anything, and then bang. For a minute I thought his truck backfired, but it had that echoey sound you hear when someone shoots on the other side of the ridge. That's why I know it had to be the shot that killed Dodge. Someone has to tell the cops. I don't think they will believe me."

"I'll talk to them," Emma promised. Though part of her doubted the police would give the story coming from her any more credence than they did Bonnie. "I heard your cousin was seen heading to Dodge's house that day. Do you know why he was going there?"

Bonnie turned her face away. When she turned back, Emma was surprised to see tears in her eyes.

"I think he might have been going to Dodge's because he was mad. Dodge he—he touched me—and then . . ." She gestured at her black eye and whispered, "He punched me."

"Are you all right? Do you want to see a doctor? I can take you."

Bonnie shook her head, wiped the tears away briskly. "No. I already went. I'm fine."

Emma wanted to say something. To call her out on the obvious lie but she knew it would be pointless, instead she asked, "Can you tell me why Dodge . . . Why he did that?"

Bonnie shook her head. "I just want you to tell the cops it wasn't Willy who killed him. You should go. I have to do homework."

Emma knew a dismissal when she heard one. There was so much she wanted to ask but Bonnie didn't seem to want any more questions. It was time to leave.

On the way back to Hollis, she decided to call John Stiles, her friend with the sheriff's office. It was late enough that he should be at work, and he was. He answered on the first ring.

"Hi John, it's Emma."

"Hey kiddo. What do you need?"

"Advice. I just got some information on the Keller

thing. Not sure what I should do with it."

"What kind of information?"

"I talked to someone who says they were with Willy Keene when Keller was killed. They heard the shot."

"Reliable someone?"

"I think so."

"Shit."

"Yeah, I know. Sort of brings everything into question."

"You need to come in and make a statement first thing tomorrow."

"I will. Who should I ask for?"

"Someone in the homicide unit. I'm not sure who. Damn, this is going to ruin someone's day."

*　　*　　*

After hanging up, John went to the break room for a cup of coffee. ADA Beale was sitting at a table, reading a magazine, a cup of coffee and an empty plate in front of him.

He looked up. "Loving these late shifts, John?" Beale asked.

John nodded. He didn't mind Beale. Unlike some of

the guys in the DA's office he wasn't known for being an ass in court, trying to win a case by attacking a cop's ethics or integrity. Besides, the guy was always friendly, chipped in for stuff, bought your kid's girl scout cookies, wrapping paper, or whatnot, without bitching about it like so many of the single guys did.

"Yeah, most of the fun happens at night, as you know. For instance, I just got a call from a local PI. She says Willy Keene couldn't have killed Dodge Keller." John delivered his news in a way that would provide the most shock value. After all, Emma hadn't actually said she had proof.

"Wha-what?" Beale said.

Modifying his statement, John said, "Well actually, she says she knows someone who is claiming they were with Keene at the time of Keller's death."

"Who is she? What exactly did she tell you?"

"Hang on, I'll get some creamer and tell you all about it," said John, taking up his coffee mug and heading for the refrigerator. "About time for me to take a break anyway."

* * *

After their talk, Beale left John as soon as he could and escaped to his office. He needed to think. Everything had been done, all the edges tucked down. Now it was all a goddamn mess. Time to straighten this shit out once and for all. Things were spiraling out of control. If he didn't take decisive steps then everything he'd worked so hard for would blow the hell up.

Long ago he'd set a goal for himself. A fat number that would assure the retirement he wanted. So few planned ahead, but he had. He'd sacrificed long enough and he was sick of crappy apartments, basic transportation.

He'd just found a house. *The* house. It was in Andorra, a sweet little town between France and Spain. A place with no extradition, not that he expected there to be a problem. He was on no one's radar and if he worked it right, never would be. He was close, so damn close. He couldn't afford anyone getting in his way, not now.

Emma Richland. She could be a problem. Funny he'd never heard of her before. According to John she'd been in business for at least three years, had an office in Hollis, and did a lot of work around the county.

Recently, she'd been investigating the warehouse fire. That's what must have put her in contact with Dodge, but why was she nosing around in his murder? Did someone hire her to do that? Who and why?

According to John, she was planning to talk to homicide in the morning. Give them a possible alibi for Willy Keene. If she did, the whole damn investigation would reopen. If somehow the police stumbled over the fact that the real killer wasn't the Keene kid but had been Jelly—if they followed that trail to him. Well, that could be a problem. Could he trust Jelly?

The Indian was something of an unknown element. Most of their dealings had been through Dodge. All he knew about him was that Dodge thought he was dependable and that he had a wife he was crazy about. Beale didn't have any sort of handle on the man. No leverage he could use to demand loyalty. Maybe he should have hired someone from out of town to take out Dodge.

"Damn it," he said to the empty room. He looked at the business card John had given him, dug out of his old Rolodex.

"They say to move our contacts onto the computer," John had told him, as he'd flipped through what had to be hundreds of cards. "But who had all the numbers last month when the power went out?" He said it with the smug tone of someone who feels they've finally been proven right.

Pulling a business card from a plastic sleeve he'd handed it over. "Don't bother getting it back to me. She gave me a few."

Picking up his office phone, Beale called the number. After three rings a woman's voice said, "Richland Investigations, can I help you?"

"Is this Emma Richland?"

"It is."

"This is Robert Beale, Assistant District Attorney. I've heard from John Stiles that you have information on Dodge Keller."

"That's right. John said I should come in first thing in the morning."

"Good. I'm handling that case and I'm a little tied up in the early morning. Could you come by at eleven?"

"Sure. Is your office—"

"Second floor of the courthouse. Just tell the receptionist you have an appointment. He'll bring you back to my office."

"Okay, I will. I'm sorry, but could you tell me your name again?" He did, and she jotted it down on the back of a junk mail envelope.

"All right, I'll expect to see you at eleven. Oh, and Ms. Richland, it would be best if you didn't discuss this with anyone but me, at least not until we've had a chance to talk. Do you understand?"

"Of course." she told him.

"Good, then I'll see you tomorrow, he said.

"Yes. Good—"

He'd hung up.

CHAPTER TWENTY-FIVE

Tuesday, September 18

Emma had twisted and turned in her sleep all night. She was nervous about her meeting with the ADA but that wasn't all of it. The girl, Bonnie, bothered her. Living way out there with her messed up mother. She wondered if she should call child services. When Bonnie said Dodge touched her, hit her, she'd asked why but as soon as the girl pushed back she let it go. Why hadn't she fought for more details?

She knew why, because she didn't really want those details. Also, she hadn't wanted to lose her focus on the investigation. Terrible excuses. She'd have to follow up and talk to Bonnie again. See if she was all right. If she didn't it would haunt her. It already was.

Giving up on sleep, she decided to get out of bed. It

was dark. The moment she threw off her covers the cold air made her shiver and reminded her that the automatic thermostat was set lower at night to save money. A decision she regretted as her bare feet made contact with the wood floor.

She hurried into the living room, bumped up the thermostat, and heard the furnace kick in. Back in her bedroom she gathered her clothes and took them into the bathroom with her. A shower would warm her up.

The hot water felt good, driving away the chill. The scent of the peppermint soap she liked helped too, bringing her fully awake. As she shampooed her hair she thought about how radically her life had changed in the last few years. Sometimes it felt as if she'd stopped making choices and allowed fate or chance to step in and take control.

When she'd learned she had a talent for investigative work, she'd followed that thread and let it take her here. When Gwen asked her to look into an arson, even though she knew it was way outside her skill set, she had said yes. When they found Dodge's body she'd let a detective's rude comments drive her to make the decision to find a killer. Now she was being driven by a phone call from a girl she didn't even know or have reason to believe. A good investigator would be more suspicious and not take Bonnie's words at face value. A good investigator would question everything. But then, she'd always fallen into the trap of trusting people. Especially Mark. She thought she'd lost that habit but maybe not entirely.

When she discovered Mark wasn't who she thought he was, it was as if everything that she believed in was wrong. It was too much and she had shattered into a million broken pieces, each sharp edged and painful.

It had taken a long time and a lot of work to glue the pieces back together. Even now she knew the repair was imperfect. She could still feel the seams, emotional scars, the damage had been done and knew she had changed, and not in a good way. Catching him in the act, exposing his lies, was supposed to be a triumph. It should have given her strength. It had done the opposite. It had made her too aware of how emotionally fragile she was.

One of the worst things was that El had been there. She'd been witness to Emma's worst moments.

She'd seen her weakness, and the depth of her vulnerability. Whenever she thought it was behind her, that she'd forgotten that bad time, seeing El served as a reminder.

Could they ever be as close as they'd been as children? They'd once shared being alone together as they traveled from base to base, new school to new school.

Then the retirement and the move to Hollis. The idea of staying in one place had been strange but it had been okay too. They'd spent some time together, learning to kayak and snow ski.

Then El had joined the Army, but that had been inevitable and Emma knew she'd be leaving soon too.

College had been okay. Her days were filled with classes and study groups, her nights with parties. She'd sent letters to El, complaining about certain professors and talking about the boys she'd met. She'd read El's letters, complaining about certain instructors and the boys she'd met. Their lives didn't seem that different.

Then she'd met Mark. Suddenly all her hours were filled. Letters and phone calls to Ellen dwindled but still, it had seemed normal.

They'd talked more when their father left for Panama. Together they decided he must have thought his girls were fine and he could now go off and have some sort of adventure.

Well, his girls weren't fine, at least not this one, thought Emma. Then, right after that: *God, you're such a whiner.*

Emma stepped under the downpour of water, tilted her face up, and let the water wash away her tears. Enough with the self-pity. What she needed was to get out of her own head and think about something more important, like work, and coffee.

After applying her makeup with more care than usual, she dried and loosely curled her hair. In the bedroom, she dressed in black slacks, black turtleneck and black boots. Looking at herself in the full length mirror she said, "cat burglar," to the empty room. Several scarves hung from the mirror above her dresser. She took a silk one with red poppies, added some hoop earrings with red beads and slipped a fat red bracelet on her left wrist. Staring into the mirror again she nodded her approval. "Better."

An hour later, Emma pulled into the empty lot in front of her office. It was still dark and the street lamps were on, their constant buzz as familiar and comforting as the sound of cicadas. The same lamps, however, also cast spooky shadows. With a sense of dread she didn't really fathom, but decided not to ignore, she checked the area before getting out of the car. There was nothing, and no one, there.

Once in her office, the familiar surroundings and the sight of the rising sun through her window, soothed her sense of uneasiness.

As usual, the first thing she did was start a pot of coffee. Then she dug her notes out of her purse, sat at her desk and began to organize them. Taking a legal pad she wrote down what she knew, as well as the questions she had.

5:30 a.m. – Rose seen driving to work.

6:00 a.m. – Audie reports seeing Norma leave Muddy Creek. Norma says she had breakfast with her daughter and had her hair done. Checked with salon and they confirm.

10:00 a.m. – Audie and witness saw Harry Olstad's

truck heading toward his house.

10:00 a.m. – Bonnie says Willy delivered firewood.

10:45 AM: Willy leaves and Bonnie hears a gunshot while he is still in view.

11:45 - 12:00 Norma passes Willy coming from the other direction as she's going home. She says he was "all over the road."

Once again Emma's timeline led to questions. Why did Rose lie about her husband being out of town? What is she hiding? Why does he work cash jobs? Green card? Criminal? Hiding from something? Rose works at the hospital. Access to drugs?

Norma's story seemed legit. Harry was in the hospital so he couldn't have been driving. His truck was in the shop. Did Audie and the man from the community center see, not Harry's truck, but one that was similar. Had to be. Harry's truck still at My Body Shop. They confirmed that when Harry called.

If the gunshot Bonnie heard *was* the shot that killed Dodge that meant he was killed around 10:45 that morning. Did the police and coroner agree?

Norma said Willy was "all over the road." Was that

because his truck is old and needs work, as Norma suggested, or was it because he'd just killed someone and was shook up? Or maybe, as an alternative to that, was he shook up because he'd just witnessed a murder? Assuming Bonnie was telling the truth, then based on the timeline, Willy would have arrived at Dodge's soon after Bonnie heard the shot.

Emma reviewed the timeline once more and came up with even more questions.

When did Rose come back to town?

Audie saw Harry's truck heading in the direction of his house. Did anyone see it after that?

Bonnie said Willy was mad about what Dodge had done to her. In a way she had provided a motive for him to kill Dodge. So why call and provide an alibi? Was she looking for attention or was she telling the truth, that she didn't want her cousin accused of something he hadn't done?

Sitting back in her chair, Emma chewed on the end of her pen. If she accepted that Dodge was killed around 10:45, and that the people she spoke with had been truthful, she could eliminate some of the people seen that morning.

Rose was at work. Norma was in Hollis. Willy was in sight of Bonnie. Harry was in the hospital. That meant none of the original four suspects had killed Dodge. Yet, someone had seen Harry's pickup. Emma rubbed at her temples, sensing the start of a headache.

It was possible that Audie might not have seen everyone who drove by that morning or, as she'd suggested, someone could have hiked in. If that was the case, the only way to find the killer would be through some lucky miracle of forensics, fingerprints or DNA that had been left behind.

If she was honest with herself, Emma knew that in all probability that was how this crime would be solved.

Still, Harry's truck being seen in the area bothered her. There was something strange there, another puzzle, and she wanted to figure it out. What shop had Harry called about his truck? Oh right, My Body Shop. She remembered thinking the name was clever. If the truck was at the body shop, then the only way it could have been seen in Muddy Creek was if someone who worked there had been driving it. How could she find out who worked there?

She went to the Oregon Business Registry and did a search for "My Body Shop." When she got to the name of the owner she sat back in her chair. What the hell?

With a dawning sense of understanding she read the name out loud. "Ernesto Padillo."

CHAPTER TWENTY-SIX
Tuesday, September 18

As Emma was reading his name, Ernesto Padillo was calling Assistant District Attorney Robert Beale. He always had mixed emotions when dealing with the man. Beale was competent and always came through with product as promised. On the other hand, he was part of the legal system and knew how to use it. There was more than one story out there about how crossing Beale had led to jail time, a longer sentence, even a disappearance or two. Given that, being up front with him seemed like the smart choice.

He dialed Beale's number.

"Hello."

"It's Ernesto."

"Yes?" said Beale, not trying to hide his surprise.

Usually their phone calls went the other direction, with Beale calling Ernesto to tell him when and where a new shipment could be picked up.

Ernesto's main product, heroin, came from Mexico, but Beale supplied him with Oxy and LSD. Of course some of Ernesto's heroin ended up with Beale. It was the sort of "gentleman's agreement" that kept the peace and the dollars rolling in. Neither wanted to screw it up.

"Got something I need to tell you. Gotta clear the air," said Ernesto.

Beale, who'd just arrived at work, got out of his chair and closed his office door before wandering back to his desk, the phone held tight to his ear. "Go ahead," he said.

"First, I want to say I appreciate how you stepped up for Natalia, paying for the funeral, giving her that check. It meant a lot to her, and my niece and nephew."

"Okay," said Beale, a question in his voice. Natalia was Miguel Padillo's widow. "You don't have to thank me," he said.

"No. I do. You didn't have to do all that. But that's

not the only reason I called. Your guy, the one in the paper last week. The one who got shot?"

"Yes," Beale said, acknowledging it was Dodge he was talking about.

"I want you to understand, it was for my brother."

"Your brother?"

"Yeah," said Ernesto. "I wanted to be straight with you. It had to be done and I had to be the one to do it. It was family, man. You get that, right?"

There was a moment of silence as Beale's mind scrambled to make sense of Ernesto's words and come to the realization that is was Ernesto, not Jelly, who killed Dodge.

"I get it," Beale finally agreed, trying for an air of calm he didn't feel.

"Good. I'll wait for your call," Ernesto said, indicating that it would now return to the way it had been, with Beale the one to initiate communications.

Beale heard the click as Ernesto ended the call. Jelly had let him believe he'd taken care of Dodge. Not exactly a lie, but close enough. What did the Catholics call it? A sin of omission. Yeah, a sin. He'd have to think about how to deal with that.

Fortunately it sounded like Ernesto found the justice he needed when he killed Dodge, that they could continue to work with each other. He'd have to keep a close eye on that. If Ernesto was trying to lull him into a false sense of security—if he intended to take him out as well?

He shook his head at the thought. Probably not. Ernesto liked money too much. Still, it was about family. People could be funny about family. Hard to know for sure. No, he'd better be on guard.

There was a knock on the door. Slipping the phone back into his pocket he said, "Come in."

Beth, one of the admin staff, stuck her head inside. "Just wanted to remind you that you have an appointment with Bill Curry this morning. Also, I'm updating the website with all the staff bios and you still haven't given me a headshot."

Beale nodded. "Thanks. I'll email it to you by the end of the day."

"Promise?"

"Cross my heart."

"Door open or closed?" she asked, standing with

her hand on the door knob.

"Open is fine," he told her.

Headshot, he thought, and fought the urge to laugh like a madman.

CHAPTER TWENTY-SEVEN

Tuesday, September 18

The phone rang, breaking the silence and making Emma jump. Sheepishly, she answered. The caller was Mrs. Carpenter, the woman El had referred to her. The one who had reacted to her abusive stepson by taking away the inheritance he'd been so eager to get his hands on. Emma applauded her method of revenge and looked forward to helping her find the missing cousin she wanted to leave her money to.

"I'll do an initial search online, see what I can find. Maybe we'll get lucky" she told her, after jotting down all the information she had provided regarding the cousin. Which was not much more than a name.

Finding a missing person Emma's favorite kind of puzzle. Even her anxiety about meeting with the ADA was pushed aside while she dove into databases and search algorithms.

The next time she checked the clock she was shocked to see she was going to be late. Grabbing her coat and purse she locked the door and rushed to her car. Fortunately the drive to Blue Spruce took only a few minutes and she lucked into a parking space near the courthouse. Still, her pace was more jog than walk all the way to the top of the wide concrete staircase. She rushed into the elevator and again checked her watch. Emma hated making people wait but she had five minutes to spare.

By the time the receptionist took her into what felt like the inner sanctum, her breathing had slowed enough that she thought she presented a calm exterior. Punctual and organized, yes, that was her.

Her scarf slid to the floor. She looked down at it lying there as if mocking her and suppressed a laugh at her own expense. Scooping it up she gave it a shake then rewound it around her neck. Punctual and organized. Right.

ADA Beale was sitting behind his desk and did one of those funny half-rising then sitting back down things. A vestige of the old standing when a lady enters the room etiquette, Emma thought, with a layer of uncertainty about how such a gesture would be welcomed in a more modern time.

"Please sit down," he said, "I'm Robert Beale, but please just call me Beale, everyone does. Thank you for coming to see me today."

Scanning the man and his office, Emma thought he fit the profile of professional and upwardly mobile white collar management perfectly. He was attractive, tall, fit, well-groomed and wore a charcoal gray suit, a starched white shirt and a burgundy tie. The kind of man who looked like he'd be most comfortable in a boardroom, at an exclusive health club, or on a golf course.

His office held the usual office things, a computer, a cup of pens, notepads, and a stack of folders. The only personal item was a framed photograph of what was probably his college soccer team. The near absence of personal items gave the impression that, at the office, his focus was solely on work.

"John tells me you have information about Dodge's murder," Beale said.

"Yes, but I was wondering, isn't this something I should take to the reservation police?"

Beale shook his head. "There aren't any. The county has a contractual agreement to provide law enforcement services. Don't worry, you're in the right place. I understand that you were investigating a possible arson and somehow discovered something related to the murder. Is that right?"

Emma nodded. Then she told him about working for Gwen and recounted her conversation with Bonnie. When she was done Beale said, "That's very interesting and we'll look into it. Of course you realize that Bonnie is a child, with a child's loyalty. How do you know she didn't make this up to protect her cousin?"

"I don't," Emma admitted. "I plan to keep looking into it though. If Bonnie heard the shot then someone else must have. I'm told the area is popular with people who like being outdoors hiking, riding horses, fishing. If I keep asking, someone, maybe someone who was up there, I don't know, paddling around in a canoe or something, will remember. It would really strengthen Bonnie's story if I could get just one more person to corroborate the time of the shooting."

"Maybe," he said, with a shrug that said he wasn't so sure. "I'm curious. Why are you so interested in this murder? Is someone paying you to look into it?"

With a wry smile Emma shook her head. "I wish. I guess finding Mr. Keller's body is part of it. It was such a shock to see that. It made me question who would do that to someone else, and why."

She didn't share that it had been an arrogant detective that had actually prodded her into action. Better that he think her choice came from compassion rather than petty anger. "I asked around and eventually was led to talk to Bonnie. If she's right about the time, and if she's being truthful, then the killer is still out there."

"That's unlikely," said Beale. "I don't usually do this, but let me help you save some time and effort by sharing what we know. Dodge Keller was the leader of a criminal organization which distributed drugs through a network of dealers in the northern part of the county. Willy Keene was hired by a rival dealer to kill him. As part of his plan, Willy set the warehouse fire, the one you've been investigating, we believe in an effort to draw Dodge there, where Willy was waiting.

"When Dodge didn't show up, Willy took the risk of hunting him down at his ranch, where he shot and killed him. His bloody shoe prints were all over the house. He then hid somewhere until he realized the police were on to him.

"At some point he decided he needed money and drove to Hollis intending to rob a store, which he did, holding the clerk at gunpoint. He didn't realize that he was under observation and was being followed. When he left the store, police from the city and the sheriff's office were waiting for him. When he saw them, he pulled a gun. Luckily, the officers were prepared, and he was shot several times before he could return fire."

"That's very sad."

"Tragic, yes. Of course the police are now trying to find the man who hired Willy. He's just as guilty, and should pay for all of this, and I'm including the death of that poor young man."

"But Bonnie's story—"

"Is probably just a story, but yes, I'm going to have someone check it out. If it turns out it's true we'll reopen the investigation. Given that, I'd like to ask you to do me a favor and stop your investigation. I appreciate this information and we'll definitely follow up on it, but I'm sure you can understand that you and the police questioning the same people could cause some issues. Leads can become—"

"I do understand," she said, cutting off his explanation. "I get it, and I'll stay out of it, for now. I will be calling Bonnie back though. I'm worried about her. I suspect she isn't going to school. She had a black eye and I'm hoping she didn't get it from her mother, or maybe some boyfriend of her mothers. Anyway, it has to be looked into and I've already talked to someone at DHS."

"I see," said Beale, allowing none of his annoyance to show. "It's too bad you had to call child services, but I'm glad you did. So few people bother to take action when they see something. You aren't going to ignore it. That takes courage."

"Oh please," said Emma, "It took a phone call."

"Maybe, but you know what I mean."

"I guess," said Emma, not totally immune to the man's charm. It was hard not to notice that he seemed interested. He held eye contact a little longer than normal, leaned toward her as they talked. But maybe she was just imagining it. Normally she would have enjoyed the attention of such a good looking man, but something about him bothered her. She wouldn't call him cringe worthy, but there was definitely something. Her gut, and all her spidey senses were tingling an alarm. "Well, I think I've told you everything. I'm sure your office will make sure someone follows up on Bonnie's story." She stood and half turned toward the door.

"Let me walk you out," he said, moving from behind his desk. It's jury selection day and," he checked his watch, "yeah, the lobby will be a mess. I'll take you out the back way."

"That would be great," she said, and let him lead her through the maze of offices to a stairway. He even walked to the ground floor with her.

"There you go," he said, opening and holding the door for her. "Now please remember, don't talk to anyone about this, or interview anyone else until I get back to you. Agreed?"

"Agreed."

"Good. I promise I'll call you soon."

Her smile was only a tightening of her lips.

He didn't seem to notice. His own smile was wide and warm and full of teeth.

Emma heard Beale pull the door shut as she stepped out onto a broad sidewalk. She found herself looking at an employee parking lot, surrounded by a tall cyclone fence, with gates set every few yards. She noticed the row of parking spaces closest to the building were marked reserved.

In that special row was a Tesla. She recognized the stylized T on the rear of the car. Immediately she searched for a sign that might tell her who the parking spot belonged to, but the spots were only identified by numbers painted on the ground.

Beale might know who parked there. Maybe she could catch him. She sprinted back across the sidewalk, grabbed the door handle and yanked. The door was locked and wouldn't budge.

She went back to the car. Dark blue, she noted. Taking out her phone she took a picture of the license plate. *You're being ridiculous.* She told herself. *How many Teslas are on the road now?* She knew the odds of this being the car the key fob belonged to was, well, maybe not astronomical but still, that kind of luck didn't happen. Dropping her phone back into her purse she headed for the gate that would bring her closest to her car.

*   *   *

Beale went back to his office, shut the door firmly and began pacing. His thoughts were moving fast. He'd have to call Leena. Tell her to fix up her act before a child services investigator showed up. Have to make sure she had food in the cupboard and that the place looked halfway decent. He'd helped a guy who owned a handyman service avoid jail time on his third DUI. The guy owed him a favor. He could fix up Leena's place in no time. All it would take was a phone call. People owing him favors was one of the best parts of being an ADA.

Hiring Leena was one of Dodge's many bad choices. Hiring Dodge was one of his. In fact, it seemed like Dodge was still screwing him from the grave.

Leena. Even her name was starting to piss him off. At least she was an easy problem to fix. Like all junkies, if she continued being a problem, a little uncut product would take care of it. If her mother died of an overdose, Bonnie would go straight into foster care.

She'd be far too busy with all the changes to worry about her dead cousin. If she did talk about him he doubted anyone would take the time to listen.

The only real problem was this Emma bitch. The woman was hot. He'd give her that. With thick chestnut hair spilling around her shoulders and a tight curvy body. Throughout their meeting she'd sat poised at the edge of her seat, giving him her full attention, and he'd liked it. He'd also liked how she responded to his explanation, politely, but reserving acceptance. He liked her bright and suspicious mind. Too bad the very thing he admired was the very thing that was going to get her killed.

Beale stopped wearing out the tread in his carpet and sat down. An idea had occurred to him. A way to kill two birds with one stone. "Or so to speak," he said to himself. Pulling out his phone, he called Jelly. "Remember that task I gave you at our last meeting?" Beale said, referencing their discussion at Redwing Trailhead. "I've spoken with the person who took care of it, and guess what, it wasn't you. What do you have to say about that?"

There was only silence.

"You need to explain why you didn't do your job."

"I didn't have to. It was already taken care of. Not the kind of thing you can do twice."

Beale smiled, amused by the explanation. "Guess not. Still, you could have said something."

"Didn't see the need."

"Took the credit though."

Again, Jelly said nothing.

"I put up with a lot from you. You gotta admit that. Who the hell else would hire someone named Jelly. Where'd you even get such a dumb ass name? You never told me that. How are we supposed to trust each other if you don't share the most basic shit like that?"

Jelly made a snorting noise. "What, are we bonding now? All you had to do was ask. It's not a special story.

"One of my foster fathers and two of his friends were playing poker and drinking beer. My foster father told me to get one of the men a beer, only I wasn't tall enough to reach the counter where they'd put them.

"They didn't help, just watched me find a step stool, one of those folding ones, and try to figure it out. After I did, one of them said I was so slow my brain must be like a traffic jam. Then the other one said, 'He ain't that thick, he's more like a traffic jelly.' Foster dad thought that was funny as hell and started calling me Jelly.

"After I left that place, I took the name with me to remind myself the world's full of men like that. Men that take away who you are and turn you into a joke. That what you want from me?"

"Of course not," said Beale. "What I want from you is what you gave Dodge, stay off the product, do the job and be loyal. That's the only way it will work. Only so far I'm not seeing the loyal part. You lied to me. That shows a definite lack of trust."

Beale waited a moment but Jelly said nothing. "There's something I need you to do. Something that will prove you're committed to this organization. I want you to get your wife to call a private investigator named Emma Richland. I want her to say she has information about the shooting of Dodge Keller. Tell her she wants to meet her at the trailhead, the same place we met to discuss that project you didn't handle."

"No," said Jelly without hesitation. "My wife isn't part of this. She doesn't know what I—"

"Don't say she doesn't know what you do. She knows. Nobody is that stupid. Besides, rumor has it you love her. There's no way you didn't tell her what you do, who you work for. That means she knows what I do and that gives her a lot of power but no involvement in my business. Sure, she'd try to keep you safe, but she'd throw me to the wolves in a heartbeat.

Unless of course, she had a reason not to, like maybe she took part in something once. Just once. That way if the police ask I can say she worked for me. I can tell them to put her on a lie detector. She won't pass and that will give the DAs office all they need. That's how the game's played. I might go down, but so would she. That's all the insurance I need. For fuck's sake, I gave you Dodge's place, made you number one in my organization, and I thought I could trust you. Asking you to do this is nothing."

Beale was practically shouting, each angry word getting louder and louder. He stopped, listened for a moment, heard no one moving in the hallway outside his door. Good, but he'd better keep it down. He took a deep, calming breath, then another.

"Okay, listen," he said in a more conversational tone. "You get Rose to make that call. You get the Richland bitch to the trailhead at eleven o'clock tonight or you pack your shit and run like hell. I need this business to run smoothly and without all the attention Dodge and his kind of bullshit draws. He rocked the boat way too much and I put up with it way too long. I won't make that mistake again."

"I will call the investigator," Jelly said.

"Were you not listening? That's not what I asked. Besides, she won't come alone to meet a man way out there. I'm not even sure she'll come for a woman, but I know there's a better chance if she thinks it is."

"Why do you want her there?"

"Why do you think?" Beale again reminded himself to stay calm, talk quietly. "I need to speak to her privately. It's a good spot for that. I don't want her to know who I am until I get a chance to talk to her directly. She found out some stuff about the job you didn't follow through on. I'm going to offer her something to help her forget."

"You plan to bribe her?"

"Hell yes. You know the saying, never met a man

that can't be fought. Never met a woman that can't be bought."

"You say so," Jelly said doubtfully.

"I do say so. Now get on it. I need her there tonight and I need you to call me back and tell me it's been set up." Beale hung up the cell phone with a stab of his finger. Slamming it down would have made him feel better. Technology was a cold bitch.

He dialed another number, listened to the ring until it was answered, then he said, "Ernesto. I need a favor."

CHAPTER TWENTY-EIGHT
Tuesday, September 18

Jelly was sitting on the front porch smoking a cigarette. Something he did only rarely, and stared at the row of roses along the fence. He took a long drag, exhaled slowly and watched the smoke curl around him. Tobacco was sacred. Tobacco smoke was protection and prayer, not much different than a Catholic crossing himself. Bad things were stirring. Choices must be made.

He heard her car before he saw it but he didn't move or look away from the roses. He wasn't ready to face her. She loved her job, loved having a home. He had to remind himself that mostly she loved him. That was what she said every time they met, every night when they touched. He would believe it—someday.

*   *   *

As she drove in, Rose saw Jelly sitting there, the cigarette in his hand moving up and down slowly, smoke trailing from the corner of his mouth. Something was wrong. She turned off the car, and pulled the keys from the ignition. She held them tight in her hand and sat up straighter. Her mantra ran through her mind. *When I am weak he is my strength. When he is weak I am his strength.*

Rose was a strong person, but she believed most of her strength came from her dedication to the man who sat on their porch, speaking to the spirits. She knew without him she'd still be the frightened child with no home she had once been. When they met he became her home, her heart. If love made you strong, then she was unbreakable.

Five minutes later she'd moved from loving and supportive to furious. "So what you're saying is, he wants me to call that investigator and ask her to meet me at Redwing Trailhead. What if I call and tell her the truth instead?" Rose asked. "How would he like that?"

Jelly shook his head. This argument was getting nowhere. He'd told Rose about Beale's demand and they'd been going back and forth ever since. "You have no idea how wide his network reaches," he explained. "He's got connections with a Mexican cartel, a biker gang out of LA, and some sort of lab in Nevada. He provides drugs to WIP, to the Padillo's and who the hell else I don't even know. He's the single biggest supplier of drugs for Eulalona County, and I wouldn't be surprised if he has distributors in other counties. Dodge only had one small piece of the pie."

"And now that's your piece. I know you did this for us, but we don't need this. This man is asking you to hurt people, to kill people. You're not that kind of man. If you were, I wouldn't have married you. Money isn't that important to us. If you do this, you could go to prison, you could die. It's too dangerous."

"If I don't it's dangerous too. I don't think saying no is healthy. Besides, I know you say money isn't important but it is. This is more than just pickups and drop offs. The money Dodge made was unbelievable. We're talking about enough that in just a few years I could quit and we'd still have enough to build a house somewhere. We could travel. I could give you the life you deserve."

"You are my life," said Rose. "You can quit now. We can leave. Go far away. As long as we're together, nothing else matters."

"It does matter. It's wearing you down. Rented houses we can get kicked out of on a whim. Shitty cars that break down all the time. Our life sucks."

"You're exaggerating."

"Maybe, a little. It's just that you deserve more. You want—"

"Don't you dare tell me what I want," Rose said in a voice that had gone dangerously soft. "Don't you use me to rationalize this. I never asked you to make a ton of money or buy me a house. I sure as hell never asked you to get involved with that man."

"That's true, but I am involved and now he wants to get you involved too. I'm not sure what to do. Leave the money out of it. I'm worried if we take off he'll send someone to find us. What if leaving isn't a choice. What if I'm trapped?"

"You mean what if *we're* trapped. Both of us, caught in some web of his making, while he sits back like a fat smug spider knowing we're stuck and helpless."

"I don't know what to do," Jelly admitted. "I don't know whether we should run or stay and try to make the best of it. One thing I do know is I'm not letting you make the call. I'm not letting you get involved."

Rose rolled her eyes. "Letting me?" she said, folding her arms she stared into the fire in the wood stove. Flames danced and the green wood she'd fed into it when they came inside hissed and snapped, a good reflection of her feelings, she thought.

"That didn't come out right," he said.

"Really?" Rose said. Jelly could feel her anger, but at least she was looking at him again.

"What I meant to say is, I think Beale has lost his mind. He's every bit as crazy as Dodge. I don't think he's going to lure that woman to the trailhead to bribe her. I think he is going to kill her."

As soon as he said it, Jelly knew it was the truth. Beale was cleaning house. He'd dealt with Dodge because he wasn't able to control him. Then, when the investigation might point to one of his men, he'd pasted a target on an innocent young man and had him killed by the police. Now, the Richland woman was causing problems. She was the last of the stepping stones on a path that could lead the police to him, and he wanted it removed. Sighing, Jelly swept a rough hand across his face.

"He's a monster," Rose said.

"He is. You're right, and that's why we're not going to stick around and help him. I hate to ask you this, but how fast do you think we can get packed?"

Rose smiled, a smile that lit up her beautiful dark brown eyes. "As fast as a herd of turtles."

"That fast?"

"Well, you know—the sex," she said, giving him a flirtatious smile.

"Oh, that."

"Yes, that."

"Have to make a call first. I have an idea."

Jelly called Leena and said, "Beale wants you to make a phone call."

Then he told her to get paper and a pen so she could write down the words exactly as he said them. With Leena, he wasn't taking chances. He dictated what she was going to say.

While he talked to her, he could hear Rose in the bedroom at the rear of the house. From the sound of the sliding closet door, and the thump of suitcases, she was moving considerably faster than a herd of turtles.

Leena called back sooner than expected. "Hey Jelly," she said her tone tentative but friendly. "The lady said sure, she'd meet me at eight-thirty tomorrow morning."

"At the Redwing Trailhead?" Jelly asked.

"Yep. Just like you said."

Rose came into the room and asked about dinner. "Do we dash, or do we dine and dash?" she wanted to know.

"Neither," said Jelly. "We have to meet the Richland woman in the morning. I figure we'll warn her and then we'll get the hell outta Dodge. What he'd said hit him and he shuddered."

"You okay?" Rose asked.

"Just someone walking on my grave."

Rose frowned. "Not if I can help it. Dancing only. What's our plan?"

"I call Beale and tell him she said there was no way she could meet tonight. The earliest she could manage would be ten tomorrow morning."

"Seems like an odd time."

"I know. I've thought about that. I'll tell him you said she had an early appointment with a client, plus she wanted to give Leena time to drive in from Muddy Creek."

"You want him to think I made the call."

"Yes. He won't be the wiser. It'll seem like we're doing just what he wants. If it works out, we should have time to drive out there, warn that woman and be out of town, long before he gets there. It's not much of a plan I guess. Pretty simple."

"Simple is good," said Rose. "Sometimes simple is the best."

"I hope so."

Next, he called Beale and told him that Emma Richland had insisted meeting at ten a.m. in the morning, and that there was nothing Rose could do to change her mind.

"It'll have to do," said Beale, accepting the change with no argument, which both surprised and relieved Jelly. He hung up and looked at Rose.

Rose nodded. Her usual good humor momentarily lost under the gravity of the situation. "You're doing the right thing, you know. It's what I expected of you."

"For a minute there . . ."

"I know. The money. No amount would make this right. You know that."

"As long as we're right with each other. That's all that really matters."

"We are much more than right. I've got all the suitcases on the bed but I suppose we could move them or . . . that couch looks sort of cozy."

*   *   *

The phone rang and Leena picked it up, expecting Jelly's voice again. Instead, it was Beale.

"This investigator, that's been sniffing around talking to you?" He made it a question.

"Yes?" said Leena.

"The bitch called child services on you. They'll do an inspection so I'm sending a guy out to fix up some stuff around your place. He's going to bring you some food too. Fill up the fridge and the cabinets. He'll look around while he's there and get you whatever you need to make them happy."

"Oh, thank you," said Leena. "I was afraid you were calling because you were upset I couldn't get that woman to meet you tonight. I hope eight-thirty isn't too early. Jelly said it was okay."

It was quiet so long Leena checked her phone to see if she'd accidentally hit the mute button.

"Hello?" she said. "Hello."

"Yeah, I'm here," said Beale. "No, that's fine. Eight-thirty tomorrow morning. That'll work for me."

Relieved he wasn't upset, Leena's thoughts drifted to the idea of a child services coming to her house. She didn't like strangers sniffing around her place but she knew she didn't have much choice. She'd been through it before.

Child services could make her life hell. Make her take classes even, though it meant missing work to attend. They didn't care what it cost people. Screw them. They pretended but she knew they weren't there to make her life easier.

Beale though, he was nice. Way nicer than Dodge ever was. That gave her an idea. Nervously, Leena giggled. "I wondered, since I did you this favor . . . "

"Don't worry. I got a delivery headed your way. That guy who's coming out to work on your place? He'll have something for you."

Leena felt her whole body relax. She hadn't realized how tense she was. Well of course, all the stuff with Bonnie and then Dodge getting killed. Of course she was tense. She'd feel better soon. In fact, she was feeling better already.

"Thank you," she said. But he'd already hung up.

CHAPTER TWENTY-NINE
Wednesday, September 19

It was cold but bright. The blue sky held not a single cloud. In the distance, Emma could see a flock of starlings rising and falling above a hay field. She had no idea why they were doing that. There was nothing she could see to disturb them. No tractor throwing a plume of dust in the air. No hawks, eagles or other birds of prey that she could see. Of course that didn't mean they weren't around.

She continued to watch them swirl, forming patterns that broke apart then came together again. A murmuration, that's what a flock of starlings was called, she remembered. She had no idea where she'd learned that. Probably Mark, who loved to watch the Discovery Channel. She rubbed her arms.

With the heater off the cold and damp was beginning to creep in. Emma considered starting the car. Or maybe she should get out and walk around a little. It would warm her up and maybe help calm her anxiety. But getting out of the car meant she'd be even more exposed. It was a little too quiet, disturbingly quiet.

The trailhead's parking lot sat near a crossing between a paved rural road and a trail that had once been a railroad line, but she hadn't seen a single car on the road, or a person on the trail, since she arrived. If Leena wanted a private place to meet, she had definitely found it. Emma hoped the information the woman had was worth it. A private meeting wouldn't normally be so unnerving, but this was about murder, and she believed the killer was still out there.

Working on the puzzle that was Dodge's murder, her thoughts strayed to Leena. Was it possible that Leena had shot him? It wasn't that farfetched. She had motive. After all, Dodge had hurt her daughter. Maybe that's what got him killed. Was she about to meet with a killer? That was an unsettling thought. She patted her purse; the outline of the gun was reassuring.

The phone call from Leena had been a little strange. She'd recognized the woman's voice immediately. Her first thought was that she must have received a visit from child services and was calling to accuse Emma of reporting her.

She expected her to say something like, "You sicced them on me. I'm a good mother." Or some such combination of anger and explanation. Instead, Leena had said, "I have information about the morning Dodge got killed. I need you to meet me tomorrow morning, at ten. I'm not comfortable talking about it over the phone."

Emma had wanted to say it was very unlikely their phones were bugged and they could talk freely, but knew better than to argue with someone so paranoid.

She could tell Leena was stressed as it was. Her words were stilted, as if she were reading from a script, or had practiced her lines several times.

"I guess I could meet you," Emma agreed. It's a long drive though so maybe a little later? Where would you like to meet? Your house or ...?"

"No. I will come to Hollis."

"Oh, well sure, if that's what you want." Emma was

relieved not to have to make the trek yet again. "So where should we meet. There are some coffee shops or restaurants where—."

"No. Too many people. I know a place. You know that rails to trails thing?"

"Sure." Emma had ridden her bike along several miles of the nearly hundred mile trail.

"It goes a long way. Out on the east side of the valley there's a place called the Redwing Trailhead. Hardly anyone goes there. You know it?"

"I think so. I've got a map of the trail and I'll look it up to be sure."

"Okay, good. I will meet you at ten tomorrow morning, at the Redwing Trailhead," she said, summing up their agreement. Then she hung up before Emma could say a word.

Now, sitting in her car, idly watching starlings, her thoughts began to roam and she found herself thinking about Leo. She remembered the thin white scar on his upper lip. Funny how concentrating on a small feature like that could slowly bring a person's face into focus. It was a technique she'd learned in PI 101. Helpful, analytical stuff. Useful if you had to remember and identify some perpetrator.

She found herself imagining she was tracing the scar with her fingertip as he stared down at her. The image was so strong she could almost feel his fingers slide through her hair, cup the back of her head.

The sound of tires on asphalt ripped her from the daydream. She looked up. A car was coming toward her. She recognized it. It was Rose Jamison's. Rose who had lied to her. Her stomach did an odd little flip. The same one it did when she was standing on a cliff looking down a great distance. The key was still in the ignition. Just in case she had to leave in a hurry, she turned the car, put her foot on the brake, and put it in gear. Reaching into her purse, she wrapped her hand around the handle of the gun, and waited.

A man was driving, Rose was in the passenger seat. The car pulled into the parking area, circled Emma's car and pulled up alongside so that the cars were facing in the same direction. Rose rolled down her window and Emma did the same. Rose said, "You have to get out of here. You've been set up. Someone is coming to kill you."

"What are you talking about? Why would someone want to kill me? Where's Leena?"

"Leena was hired to get you out here."

"Who hired her?"

Rose hesitated, turned to the man in the front seat then back to Emma. "I can't tell you that. Only that he doesn't like you investigating. He's a bad man, a crazy man, but also a very powerful one. We agreed to warn you but we can't tell you too much. If he finds out we named him we know he'll come after us. He might anyway. We're leaving. You should too. Go far away, to another town, another state."

"You're trying to scare me."

"Yes. I'm trying to scare you. I'm scared. My husband has given up everything so we could save you. Don't waste it."

Rose was half turned in her seat, her right hand grasping the pillar between the front and side window of the car. Her grip tightened and her knuckles went white. "Please, they think the meeting is at ten." She twisted her wrist to look at her watch. "You don't have much time. Go home, pack and run. He may not follow you to your house, but I wouldn't count on it."

"But you won't tell me who he is?"

"No." Rose said, shaking her head from side to side.

"Then I'll have to call the police," Emma said, hoping the threat would change Rose's mind.

"Yes, that's very wise," Rose said unexpectedly. "Call them now. But do it as you're driving away from this place."

"Why are you doing this?"

"I told you. I don't want you to die. I don't want anyone to die."

"We have to go." The man in the front seat, who Emma assumed was Rose's husband, Charles or Jelly depending on who you asked, had finally spoken.

"I know," Rose said to him. "Emma, please believe me." She wore a pleading look that was hard to mistake. Emma knew Rose truly believed what she was saying. Her life was in danger.

Suddenly Rose's car leapt forward, dust and gravel pinging off Emma's Jeep as it skidded a little in the dirt and gravel. When it bounced onto the asphalt the driver hit the gas even harder and the little car sped away. Emma watched it disappeared over the horizon.

She let go of the gun, took her hand out of her purse, and wiped her palm on her jeans. Then she put her hand on the steering wheel. *Time to go.* Taking her foot off the brake, she let the car roll across the parking area and onto the road, where she accelerated gradually. She would call El, talk to her about what she should do next. Calling the police was high on her list. But first she'd call El.

Reaching into her purse she felt around for the familiar rectangle of plastic.

The car came from behind and it came fast. She hadn't seen it when she pulled onto the road. She wasn't traveling nearly as fast as it was but she wasn't concerned. There was no oncoming traffic. The driver could easily go around. Only he didn't.

In disbelief, Emma saw the old car, as big as a whale in her rearview, coming right at her. It slammed into her rear bumper. Her car was jolted and she was whipped forward then back. Her car skidded toward the ditch that ran along the side of the road. She fought the wheel, stood on the brakes, but it wasn't enough. The front wheels bumped off the asphalt and into deep gravel, where they sank. The rear of the car spun, a motion that pushed Emma to her right, powerless against the centrifugal force. Only the seat belt kept her from sliding out of her seat. Then the car came to a sudden stop, rocking from side to side.

Her purse had been swept to the floor of the passenger seat. Most of the contents were lying there, including her gun. She lunged for it but the seat belt, forgotten in her panic, kept her pinned, her fingertips mere inches away.

Sitting up, she had just managed to press the release button, when a strong pair of arms reached through the window, grabbed her and dragged her out.

She kicked, punched and screamed. Her attacker's hands slipped and he dropped her to the ground. She rolled to her side and kicked out, catching his knee hard. She heard him suck air between his teeth, and grunt at the pain. Then he was reaching for her and she was scrambling away, trying to get to her feet and run.

As she reached her feet, she was startled as another man, this one with red hair, clutched her shirt. She heard fabric tear. He changed his grip, letting go of her shirt and grabbing her hair instead. Pulling her back against him, he kept one hand wrapped in her hair, the other around her throat.

Panting from exertion and fear she could smell his cologne and his sweat. As she struggled to break free, and tried to stomp on his foot, the man who had pulled her from the car kicked her legs out from under her, dropping her hard on the ground once more. They piled on and pulled her arms behind her. She felt something slipped around her left wrist and then around her right. There was a zzzt sound and her wrists were pulled together. They were using zip ties she realized and her terror reached another level.

Ferociously, she kicked at the men holding her, hoping to break a kneecap if she were lucky. She wasn't. Her kick missed but one of theirs didn't. A steel toed boot slammed into the back of her knee. She rolled onto her side in agony.

The redheaded man pressed his boot against the back of her neck, pushing her face into the gravel. When he finally let up she turned and spat out small bits of gravel and dirt. She could taste blood on her tongue. She hadn't landed a single blow.

They lifted her from the ground, pulling her wrists

so high she was sure they would tear her arms from their sockets. The pain made her eyes water. The tears running down her face adding to her fury.

She was able to see enough to note that her car was facing the wrong way and sat half in the ditch. Behind it was the car that had hit hers. A monstrous old thing with a metal plate welded on the front and destruction derby dents, like bruises on a prize fighter, that spoke of past encounters. Emma was certain this wasn't the first time they'd done this.

A truck was coming down the road towards them. It pulled up alongside and stopped. Emma realized it was a tow truck and knew whoever was driving it wasn't there to help her. He got out and came around the truck. He looked Latino. "Take it to the shop?" he asked, directing his question to the man who had been driving, also Latino.

Two men who both looked Mexican-American. The shop. She thought about what Rose had said. The man she was afraid to name. It had to be Ernesto Padillo. He had access to cars and a tow truck. He owned the shop where Harry's truck was. It was all coming together. She had too try something. Anything.

"I already called the police. They know all about your boss, Ernesto Padillo. They know about your drug operation. They know you had Dodge killed. Your best bet is to cut ties with him and run. You don't want to be caught in the middle of committing a crime when the cops get here."

They ignored her and pushed her toward their car. With her first step she almost fell, as pain shot through her damaged knee. Too soon, the reality of that pain was not as bad as the reality of what they were going to do. One of them released her long enough to open the trunk.

She fought again, turning her head and reaching with her teeth, eager to get a bite of skin, tear into flesh, grind her teeth into bone. She kicked too, ignoring the pain from her knee that was like a constant scream.

Fighting didn't matter. They simply lifted her off her feet, and threw her into the trunk with as much care as if she were a flat tire. One of them put his hand around her ankle and pushed her foot, which was dangling outside, into the trunk. She hated the touch of his fingers on her skin. Hated more the sound of the trunk slamming as she was locked in.

As her eyes adjusted, she tried to look around the dim space for a way out, for a weapon. There was nothing. The trunk was empty. Coarse carpeting scratched her skin. Above her was only the metal interior of the trunk. She felt around for a release. It was there but when she tugged on it she realized it wasn't connected. Could she kick out a tail light. She saw narrow bands of light and dark and realized metal bars had been welded across them. Yes, they had done this before.

There was a lurch as the car accelerated. Trying to straighten her legs, she found the width of the trunk forced her to keep her knees bent. The injured knee had stopped screaming and was now only moaning with every beat of her heart.

She fought to catch her breath. Hard to do in the still air of the trunk. It smelled of oil and gas and helplessness. She wondered how many others had shared this ride, felt this terror.

For the first few minutes she tried to formulate a plan. Then she resorted to praying. "I know you're probably not real but, if you are, if you could do something. I need help." Her whispered plea brought fresh tears of fear and frustration.

Why hadn't she taken El with her, or Leo. Because I shouldn't need them, she answered herself. *But you did. You do.* Fresh anger momentarily conquered fear and she began kicking at the sides of the trunk. The sound was much less than she'd hoped. Time passed in fits and starts. It seemed like it was taking hours but it might have been minutes.

She tried to free her hands. An article she'd read said it was possible to break free of zip ties. Sadly, the article only talked about what to do if your hands were tied in front of you, not behind your back. If she ever got out of here she'd have a word with whoever had written that useless garbage.

Emma struggled to slide her wrists down to her ankles so she could step through and bring them to the front. She couldn't do it. Sweat dripped into her eyes as she tried. The pain in her knee was too much to fight against.

Giving up on escape, she pushed herself into the trunk as far back as she could. Maybe she could at least get in a few good kicks.

Suddenly, she was thrust toward the front of the trunk. Time was up. The car had stopped.

CHAPTER THIRTY
Wednesday, September 19

When the trunk was lifted the influx of cool, fresh air was wonderful. The light made her dark-adapted eyes sting. Once again tears pricked her eyes and one slid down her cheek.

"Get out of there," someone barked at her sharply.

She didn't move except to close her eyes, pretending to be unconscious. As soon as one of them got close enough ...

The man she thought had been the driver of the car that hit hers, reached inside the trunk. He took a handful of her shirt, and tried to pull her out. Spinning on her hip, she broke free, then kicked out with both feet, feeling a rush of satisfaction as she connected with his face.

He yet out a yelp and stepped back. She struggled to climb out, but before she was able to reach the edge of the trunk he was back with the redhead.

The two of them grabbed her by her arms and legs and dumped her on the hard concrete floor. The one she'd kicked had a thin line of blood dripping down his chin. He looked like he was drawing his foot back to kick her, when a third man appeared.

The new man, Latino like the driver, wore a gray cap with a Corvette emblem. He reached down, took her wrist, and easily pulled her to her feet.

Emma looked around frantically, searching again for a weapon, some way to escape. There were three of them in total. Maybe that wasn't too many. Maybe it was. It didn't matter. She wasn't going to give up.

They were inside a garage. Emma realized it must be "My Body Shop". The walls were cinder brick. The floor was concrete, stained with what she hoped was only oil and gas. There were three bays, each with a closed roll-up door. The space was brightly lit by rows of fluorescent lights hanging from the ceiling. There were rolling tool boxes and shelves against the walls filled with cans and bottles. The only car in the garage was the one they clearly used for kidnapping people. A different kind of bodywork all together, she thought, amazed at her morbid sense of humor at such a serious time.

The man in the Corvette hat stood with his hand wrapped firmly around her left arm, just above the elbow. The other two stood facing him, clearly awaiting orders. The man's obvious sense of authority told her she was in the presence of Ernesto Padillo.

Padillo had a large squat nose set in a long face, deep set eyes that drooped at the outer corners and a gap between the whitest teeth she'd ever seen.

The one she thought of as the driver was middle aged, clean shaven, with short hair, pock-marked cheeks and dried blood on his chin.

The tall redhead had a scruffy beard and what looked like chewing tobacco stains at the corners of his mouth. He'd been the one who put his boot on the back of her head. There was no blood on his face but she'd have loved to put some there.

Looking up at the man holding her arm she asked, "Are you Ernesto Padillo?"

He gave her a cold smile that didn't reach his eyes and nodded. "Si," he said, curtly. "You know that I am."

"Is this about me looking into Dodge?" she asked.

"Dodge. Pendejo," the man hissed in her ear. "I blew his fucking head off. It exploded like a goddamn melon. It was way too good for him. He should have died slow. I should have brought him here."

He tightened his hold. She could feel his fingers digging into her arm, wanted to pull away, but decided not to resist. Is he thought she'd given up. Or if he thought she was timid, fearful, maybe she could catch him off guard. When he started across the bay, pushing her ahead, she exaggerated her limp, practically leaning on him for support. He'd killed Dodge. He was going to kill her. If he gave her the smallest glimmer of a chance she would take it.

"Get the lift down," he said. The redhead moved into a slow jog, while the other man followed more slowly.

The redhead reached the farthest bay, and Ernesto prodded her in that direction. In that bay was a lift. A huge blue steel machine with two vertical posts and a cross piece at the top.

The redhead grabbed a black box at the end of a thin yellow hose that wound like a slinky and was connected to one of steel posts. He pushed a button with his thumb and as she watched the posts lowered, sinking into themselves until the cross piece was about six few feet from the ground.

With a sound too much like a whimper, Emma stepped back, pulling Padillo with her. He tightened his grip, grabbed her hair with his free hand and held her. "Jorge, the rope."

Jorge went to one of the tool carts, and removed a length of rope.

Emma kicked backward, driving the heel of her boot into Padillo's leg then sliding it down his shin. The moment she felt his grip loosen, she spun away and facing him did a front kick. He was bent forward, reaching for his injured leg and the toe of her boot caught him under the chin, snapping his head back. She turned and ran.

The sound of traffic outside was tantalizingly close. If she could get out and get to the traffic . . .

Sprinting across the garage her mind scrambled for an escape route. She didn't know how to make the big garage-style doors go up, but she'd spotted a standard door near the corner farthest from the empty bay. It had a window inset at the top and sunlight made a bright white square against the blinds hanging in front of it, as though it were a beacon urging her to reach it.

Almost there. She could hear them coming, their shoes slapping against the concrete, their breathing loud. Everything began moving slowly while her perceptions grew. Her senses were wide awake and focused on the door ahead, the light, the door handle. Her hands were still tied behind her but she pictured how she would do it. How she would slow down, turn, grab the handle and turn it with both hands.

Intense pain exploded from her ankle and she was knocked down like a bowling pin. She caught a glimpse of a tire iron spinning nearby, heard the metallic clank and rattle as it hit and skittered across the pavement.

The impact took her feet out from under her, knocked her over backward. She landed on her elbows. Barely slowing, she rolled to her feet.

The redhead tackled her, slamming her into the door. It shook from the impact. She spun and tried to drive her forehead into his but missed. He shoved his forearm into her throat, driving her back. The back of her head slammed into the wall near the door. Sparks of light bloomed, while the edges of her sight went dark. She felt her knees give way, but no pain, as she was operating on adrenaline and fear.

The next thing she heard was panting breaths. It took her a moment to realize it was her own panicked breathing. They had her again, one on each side, their arms supporting her as if they were drinking buddies helping a pal. She helped the illusion, staggering like a drunk.

They lifted her higher, half carrying, half dragging her toward their boss. The straps around her wrists dug into her skin. The toes of her boots slid across the concrete. Waves of helplessness seemed to accompany the waves of pain that finally reached her. Her knees and elbows throbbed and there was something very wrong with her ankle. When she tried to straighten it she almost screamed.

They dragged her back to the lift and stopped underneath it. Ernesto was there, waiting. A noose had been tied to the cross bar and now dangled at his side.

He was bleeding. A slender line of red tricking down the corner of his mouth. Despite her fear, she felt pleased to see she'd hurt him. She lifted her head and stared into his shark-black eyes again.

He wiped his mouth with the back of his hand, which smeared blood across his face, making him look primitive and fierce.

Looking down, he saw the blood on his hand and stared back at her with an expression of pure malice. He opened his mouth and pointed to his teeth. "You broke my tooth bitch. Going to cost me money. Going to cost you too."

Stepping forward, he grabbed the noose and slipped it over her head. She felt the stiff rope against her skin.

"Bring it up, Jorge," he said.

Emma had been taught that if she ever found herself in a hostage situation she should try to humanize herself. "Get them to use your name," the instructor had said. "You want them to see you as a person, to talk to you. "

The problem was that Ernesto *was* talking to her, not because he was starting to see her as a person, but because she had hurt him. He was angry and he wanted to talk, but only in order to taunt her.

"Bring it up slow, real slooow," he said. dragging out the word. "You know what happens to people who get hung slow?" he asked, a gleam of cruelty dancing in his dark eyes. "They mess their pants. A truly shitty way to go." He laughed, his eyes now twinkling with humor and something darkly sadistic.

"Chinga tu madre," Emma said. Fuck your mother. It was the first, and nearly all, the Spanish she'd learned. "You're a stupid pig. So stupid you let your own brother get killed."

"You don't know nothing, bitch."

"If I don't know anything, then what the hell am I doing here?"

"You're here because you pissed off the wrong person. Because you can't stop digging into shit that's none of your business. He warned me you would be trouble."

"He who?" The realization that Ernesto wasn't in charge surprised her. "You have a boss. Who is it?"

"If I told you I'd have to kill you." He laughed again, so hard he had to wipe away tears.

"Tell me," she said. "Tell me who your boss is?" The need to know was so intense she stepped forward. The rope around her throat tightened. She took a step back, closer to the center of the beam. It relieved the tension for a moment, but the posts had begun to rise, lifting the bar the noose was tied to.

It continued to rise, the knot tied to form the noose began to press against her jaw, pushing her head up and back. Then, it stopped. Jorge had taken his thumb off the button.

The rope held Emma erect, almost on tiptoe.

"What are you doing?" Ernesto asked Jorge.

"You told me to go slow."

"Slow, not stop. Keep going. I want to see this bitch beg. Come on now, you ask nice, maybe you'll live a little longer."

Feeling the noose tighten, knowing she would soon be unable to talk she stared into Ernesto's eyes and with all the courage she could muster she said, "Fuck you."

CHAPTER THIRTY-ONE

The door that Emma had been so desperately trying to reach didn't swing open, it burst open. The window exploded, sending glass shards flying.

Leo had taken one of the wheels he'd found stacked in front of the garage and used it as a makeshift battering ram. Now, he dropped the wheel, fell to his knees in the doorway, and went for his gun.

Ellen, gun in hand, stepped around him into the garage, took cover behind a tool box and looked for a target.

All three men ran, fumbled for their guns, tried to get to the battering ram of a car and use it as a shield.

The redhead made it first, Jorge close behind. Ernesto, because he was closest to Emma, was Ellen's primary target. She caught him as he was turning to run, pulling his gun from a shoulder holster. Three bullets, closely spaced, and he dropped to the ground and stayed there.

Leo fired under the car. The bullets hit the hard concrete and whined, ricocheting toward the far wall.

Someone cursed. Ellen used the moment and Leo's cover fire to run to Emma. She was struggling, the noose cutting off her air as the lift continued to rise. Her eyes were wide and desperate.

"Lo-o," she gasped. Ellen couldn't understand what she was saying but Emma had turned her back to her. Her tied hands were clasped, both forefingers pointing.

Ellen saw it then, the controller for the lift, lying on the ground at Emma's feet. Three buttons! She wasn't sure which one to press.

Stop. Think.

She stared down at the controller. Three fat buttons in a row, red, white and black. The buttons were worn and dark with grease. She brought the controller closer to her face, caught the faint outline of an arrow. White arrow up. Black arrow down.

Down!

She pressed the black button. The posts stopped. Emma was choking. Ellen could hear her. Then the sound was drowned by a fresh burst of gunfire. Ellen ignored it and held the button down with every bit of pressure she could muster. Slowly, the posts began to slide downward. Dropping the controller, Ellen got her fingers around the rope, loosened the noose and lifted it from around her sister's neck.

As soon as she was free, Emma fell to the ground. Her injured ankle unable to bear her weight.

Ellen shoved her gun in its holster, took her sister's hand, and pulled her to her feet.

Emma, her arms still tied behind her, struggled to help. The sound of gunshots filled the enclosed space. Emma had taken two lurching steps, leaning heavily on Ellen, when, suddenly, Leo was there.

He reached for Emma as Ellen drew her gun and started peppering shots toward the men still hiding behind the car.

Sweeping Ellen up, Leo ran for it. Fragments of concrete exploded around them. Ellen dropped to one knee and searched for a target. One of the men popped up from behind the car. She fired and heard a yelp.

Leo and Emma burst out of the garage and into bright sunlight. Leo shoved Emma to the side, turned, aimed toward the car but held his fire, waiting for his eyesight to adjust.

Ellen, hunched to make herself a smaller target, scuttled through the door, then swung and fired her last three rounds at the back wall. Shattered bits of masonry rained down.

Staying low, she did a fast crawl to the side, dropped to a crouch and reloaded, ejecting the empty magazine and slapping in another.

It was quiet.

Emma sat with her back to the wall, her good leg drawn up, the injured one stretched in front of her. The throbbing in her ankle made her hope she wouldn't have to move again soon.

Ellen watched the door as Leo reloaded. Then she pulled a knife from her pocket, opened it and carefully cut through the ties around Emma's wrists.

Relieved to be free, Emma brought her hands to her lap and tried to rub life back into them. They had fallen asleep, and the initial tingle turned into pinpricks of pain as blood rushed to her fingers. She didn't mind. The pain was nothing compared to the rush of being free.

"Wait until they try to come out and shoot them?" Ellen asked.

"Maybe we call the cops?" suggested Emma. "They can deal with them."

Leo didn't offer an opinion, just remained where he was, his attention on the doorway.

"How d-did you f-find me?" Emma asked, a combination of pain and adrenaline making her voice shake. "H-how did you know where I was?"

"I put a tracker on your phone," said Ellen in an offhand way, as if it were an everyday occurrence.

"You what? How?"

"Remember that day at your office when I put Mrs. Carpenter's name in your phone? Well, before I did that, I loaded a tracking app on your phone. I was worried about you. I knew once you started investigating this murder you wouldn't let it go."

Emma took a deep, shuddering breath and thought about it a moment before saying, "That was very sneaky of you. Good thing it saved my ass or I'd be furious."

Ellen smiled. "Yeah, I noticed this morning that you, or at least your phone, were out in the middle of nowhere. It made me nervous, so I talked to Leo and we decided to see if we could find you."

"I'm not sure I'd say *we* decided." said Leo.

Ellen shot him a look, then said, "Oh my god. You're bleeding!"

Leo shrugged, then looked down at his arm and nodded. "That happens when you get shot."

Emma looked at Leo, saw what Ellen had seen first. Blood was steadily dripping from the fingertips of Leo's left hand.

"I'm good," he said. He stood up slowly, reaching out once to steady himself, leaving a bloody palm print on the wall.

Seeing this, Emma said to her sister, "To hell with waiting for those bastards to come out. Call 911."

CHAPTER THIRTY-TWO
Wednesday, September 19

When the police arrived, sirens blaring, Emma took what felt like her first full breath since being hit and run off the road. The first ambulance took Leo away. Soon after another showed up and she was quickly, and with no argument from her, whisked off to Melvin Morgan Memorial in Blue Spruce.

After arriving, she wondered what all the hurry had been about. For more than an hour, she'd been sitting in a back room in her underwear and a drafty hospital gown. This was not good for someone with no patience. Though it did gave her plenty of time to worry about Leo. All she could hope for was that the wait meant everyone was busy taking care of him. That was a sacrifice of time she was willing to make.

The police arrived before the doctor. Awkwardly she tugged at her dressing gown and did her best to answer their questions. Much of the interview seemed to take place in a fog of pain and anxiety. Her mind was far away. Finally they seemed satisfied and left, though not before telling her to come in and give a statement as soon as she was able.

A doctor finally showed up, shook her hand and introduced herself. She took a quick look at her various injuries, poked, prodded and made her move things in ways that were not comfortable. Then she said she'd order x-rays. When Emma asked about Leo she shook his head and said, "Another doctor is looking at him," and then she left.

Another wait, a little shorter this time, before the doctor returned. Ignoring Emma, she sat in a rolling chair, opened a monitor, looked at it without expression, hit a few keys, looked some more and then spun her chair to face her.

"Let's see. You have a bump on your forehead and possibly a mild concussion. It's not severe so bed rest, fluids, ice for the bump and take some ibuprofen.

"There is some bruising and a few minor scratches

on your neck, but we'll clean them up and get you some antibiotic cream.

"The knee is going to take the longest to heal. I'm pretty sure it's a sprain but we'll see how it goes and I might order an MRI.

"The ankle is a bruised Achilles tendon. You'll need to wear a boot for a month or more. I was worried about a tear but it looks pretty good and we want to keep it that way. I want you to follow up with your own doctor and let him know if you develop a headache, or feel nauseous or dizzy. Do you have all that?"

Emma nodded. "Can I get dressed now?" She was more concerned with Leo than with her minor bumps and bruises. All she wanted was to get out of this room and find him.

The doctor gave Emma her first smile. "Not yet. I'll send a nurse in to bandage your knee and show you how to strap your foot into the boot. She'll also talk to you about crutches or a cane. You're lucky the injury to your knee and ankle are on the same leg or you'd be going home in a wheelchair. I know you've been through a traumatic experience, so the nurse will also have a list of local counseling services. Do you have any questions?"

Emma shook her head. "No, I'm good."

"Great. Take care of yourself."

The minute she was out of the room, Emma scooted to the end of the bed and pulled up the bag of her clothes that they'd hung there. She tore off the gown and quickly put on her bra and struggled into her blouse. Then, so as not to waste time, she managed to get her good leg into one leg of her pants.

She was sitting there, mostly dressed, when the nurse showed up. Maybe her sense of urgency helped the nurse move faster. In any case, she was bandaged, booted, and had her release paperwork in hand in minutes.

"You'll want a cane at least," the nurse said, handing her a wooden cane with a rubber tip.

Emma found that, with its help, she could walk, albeit slowly, and she proved it for the nurse.

"Here are some lists of physical therapists and counselors, your prescriptions, and an after care packet," the nurse said. "Make sure you call a physical therapist as soon as possible."

Emma took the multiple sheets of paper she'd been given, folded them in half and shoved them in her back pocket.

"Now I'll go get a wheelchair and we can get you out of here."

"Okay," said Emma brightly, and as soon as the woman was out of sight, limped into the hallway and down the corridor to the elevators.

Eventually she made her way to the ER registration desk and asked if Leo Vargus had been admitted. The nurse checked, then said, "Are you a family member?"

"I'm his sister," she lied.

"Well then, Mr. Vargus was treated and released."

"So he wasn't hurt badly."

"I don't think so."

Unexpectedly, dark gray shadows gathered on the edges of her vision. Emma's legs felt weak and she wobbled, then abruptly sat in one of the chairs in front of the receptionist's desk.

Bent forward, cupping her face in her hands she tried not to faint. As if from nowhere, her own invisible man, Leo, appeared beside her. She felt his arm go around her shoulders. Smelled the cologne he wore. El was there too, stroking her hair, asking if she was all right.

She took a deep breath and the darkness was gone. "I'm fine, I'm good," she said, and it was the truth. "I guess it hit me all of a sudden. Getting kidnapped. Almost hung. Shot at. You getting shot," she said, looking up at Leo. "Can you guys take me home?"

"I can call a taxi to take us all home," said Ellen, and Emma realized that she had no idea where her Jeep was.

Once in the taxi, they decided to go to Ellen's house. The house had belonged to their father but when he decided to leave for Panama he'd left it for the girl's use, to live in or rent, he'd told them.

After Mark, Emma had no desire to live with someone and said no thanks. Ellen, with no desire to look for an apartment, had moved in. Given that she carried all her worldly belongings in two large duffel bags, it hadn't taken long.

"I think you should stay in the guest room until you're better," Ellen said. The guest room had once been Emma's. The familiarity might be comforting.

When they arrived at the house, Leo asked the cab to wait while he helped Emma inside.

"Stay here with your sister," he said to her. "She's been really worried about you. I'm going to go home, get a shower, change clothes and get my car. I'll be back in a few hours."

"You sure you're okay to take a shower by yourself?" Emma asked innocently. It was only when she saw her sister roll her eyes that she realized the unintentional double entendre in the question. "I m-mean, are you feeling okay?"

"He's fine," Ellen said, and continued to tease her sister. "I'm sure he can shower without your help. The bullet just grazed his forearm. Nothing vital was damaged."

"Nothing vital?," said Leo, sounding aghast. "You call this beautiful mocha skin not vital? I'll have you know there are women in many countries who would fight you on this."

"Here we go," said Ellen.

Emma lay back on the couch and closed her eyes. Safe. She was safe. The sound of Leo and El's voices like warm water, soothing her frayed nerves.

Her thoughts drifted to the conversation they'd had in the taxi on the way here.

Ellen, who had stayed at the scene talking to the police while Leo and Emma were transported to the hospital, shared what she'd learned.

"Ernesto is dead. The police told me it looked like the other two men climbed out of a bathroom window and took off. They're looking for them but," she shrugged. "The cops think they're connected to a Mexican cartel, so I'm guessing they've got the resources to get away clean."

Maybe," said Emma. "Then again, they didn't seem all that smart."

"What I don't understand," continued Ellen, "is what in the actual fuck is going on? I mean, you were looking into an arson and sort of tripped over a murder and drug dealers. I thought this Willy kid was the killer and the case was solved."

"You got some 'splainin' to do, Lucy," said Leo.

Emma brought them up to date on her investigation. At least the main points. She knew they'd want to go over it all again in greater detail. That would have to wait for later. She was tired, exhausted, plus, the pain killers were starting to kick in.

Sleep was at the end of a narrow tunnel that her thoughts kept sliding toward, thoughts about the investigation, the puppet master who was still out there, pulling strings, moving pieces. No, that was a chess master. Pawns, that what chess masters moved. Poor little pawns like her, like Willy, like Bonnie.

Her eyes snapped open and Emma sat up.

"What is it?" Ellen asked.

"I forgot about Bonnie."

CHAPTER THIRTY-THREE
Wednesday September 19

When Ellen called to say they couldn't reach Leena on her phone, and were going to drive out to Jansen's Mill, Leo had rushed over.

While he drove, Emma had filled them in on all she knew about Bonnie. The girl's belief in her cousin's innocence. Her terrible home life. The guilt Emma felt for not taking some kind of action, maybe even taking Bonnie out of there. She'd do that now. Take Bonnie home, at least for now, at least until she knew she was safe. If Leena got in the way she was more than sure El or Leo could handle her. Once she got them to buy in. *If* she could get them to buy in. It wasn't looking so good.

When Emma told her what she planned to do, Ellen said pretty much what she expected. "She's not your responsibility. Lots of kids have tough lives."

"But what if, by telling me that Willy didn't kill Dodge, she made the wrong people angry?"

"You've had a really rough day. You're seeing monsters under the bed," said Ellen.

Emma wondered if her sister was thinking of her breakdown. Was she calling her crazy?

Before she could respond, Leo, sensing the growing tension said, "Let's just get out there and see how she is. We'll decide from there."

Emma turned to Leo to respond. That was when she had seen the smoke, hanging like a dark curtain in the distance, and knew. She didn't want to know, was afraid to say anything in case the words somehow magically created a reality she didn't want. Maybe, like Schrödinger's' Cat, if she didn't look inside the box . . .

Even in Leo's Dodge Charger, with him ignoring the speed limits and pushing the sleek machine as much as he dared, it took forever to get there. Finally, they reached the road to Jansen's Mill. Leo slowed down, pulled off the highway and onto the side of the dirt road, then stopped the car.

"I can't drive this car up that," he said, as he took in the deep ruts and rocks in the unmaintained road. "She's too low slung. We'd get stuck. I'm sorry."

"It's okay," Emma told him, putting her hand on his arm. "You got us this far."

They got out of the car. No one questioned Emma or suggested she stay behind. Instead they bracketed her between them. Leo, offered her his arm while Ellen put her arm around her waist. The eerie ululations of police and fire sirens echoed from the surrounding hills.

On the highway, traffic sped by unconcerned, tires hissing on the asphalt like massive angry snakes. As they drew closer they saw lights reflected off the trees, a visual metronome flashing red, blue, red, blue.

The sun was beginning to set, changing the color of the forest, bright greens in daylight, but now with shadows like dark stains rising from the ground.

On the horizon, dark pink and orange clouds stretched across the sky like torn banners, announcing something grim, and final.

Trudging forward, Emma finally saw what she'd been dreading. Fire had turned Leena and Bonnie's home into a pile of dark rubble, framed with thin sheets of seared metal. Their twisted shapes, standing like strange abstract art, were evidence of the heat of the fire. A rainbow in the fire hose spray, faded with the sun. Water dripped from every surface and created vapor that hovered like fog.

The wind changed, blowing the smoke toward them. It was thick with the musty smell of charred wood, and the sweet scent of melted insulation. Beneath those was something else. Emma brought her hand up to cover her nose and mouth. She turned to Leo and said, "Will you ask?"

His expression was grim, jaws clenched.

Ellen squeezed Emma's shoulder and they watched as Leo walked toward the group of neighbors, who were clustered near the scene.

When he returned he looked at Emma, then at the ground, and said, "They say two bodies were carried out on stretchers. It might not have been Bonnie."

Emma shook her head. She knew better. It was okay to speak now. The spell had been broken.

"She told me she heard the shot, that it couldn't be Willy. I wasn't sure I believed her, but I should have.

Ernesto told me he did it. He said, 'I blew his head off.' He told me the truth, and so did Bonnie."

"And you'll share that truth with the police," said Ellen. "You did what you set out to do. You found the person who killed Dodge. You also did what Bonnie asked you to do. Prove her cousin was innocent."

"The only thing they have is my word that he said what he said."

"They'll believe you. You have nothing to gain by lying. Besides, maybe they'll find the shotgun he used in that garage. Maybe they'll find a lot more. Like you said, it wasn't the first time they've done something like this."

"Even if they do believe me, that's not the end of it," said Emma.

"It is," said Leo. "Ellen ended it when she killed Ernesto."

Emma shook her head stubbornly. "No, she didn't. I know Ernesto killed Dodge. He bragged about it. He also talked about someone else, someone who warned him that I'd be trouble. I think that's the person who is responsible for everything, the drugs, the arson, Dodge."

"This fire?" asked Ellen.

"Was no accident. Ernesto's boss did this. He killed them. He murdered Leena and Bonnie.

"Then it's not over," said Leo.

"Not by a long shot."

AUTHOR

Pamela Cowan is a Pacific Northwest author best known for her contemporary crime novels. Cowan is the author of the Storm series which includes *Storm Justice, Storm Vengeance and Storm Retribution*, books which follow probation officer, Storm McKenzie, on her single-minded quest for justice. She is also the author of two stand-alone novels based in fictional Eulalona County, Oregon, *Something in the Dark* and *Cold Kill*.

If you enjoyed this novel please leave a review. Reviews are invaluable to both readers and authors. It's how we find each other.

Learn more about Pamela's novels and short fiction at pamelacowan.com